the SISTER

Angeline Trevena

Bogus Caller Press

ISBN: 978-0-9934864-5-6

Cover art by Oliviaprodesign

Published by Bogus Caller Press
www.boguscallerpress.co.uk

Publisher's note:
The Sister is a work of fiction. All names,
characters, and places are the product of the
author's imagination, used in fictitious manner. Any
resemblances to actual persons, places, locales,
events, etc. are purely coincidental.

ALSO BY ANGELINE TREVENA

Cutting the Bloodline

The Paper Duchess Series:

The Bottle Stopper

The Matching

The Visionary

The Mothers

The Memory Trader Series:

The Smudger

PART ONE

1

KIOTO

I scratched at the back of my head again, my mass of curls feeling uncommonly heavy in the heat. I wasn't designed for the summer, and I certainly wasn't designed to be sat in the middle of a stifling city in the summer. I ached for the cool ocean breeze, the fresh, salty air. Instead I had the scent of substandard coffee and fat burning under a grill.

Narata frowned at me. "Why don't you just tie it up?" she asked. She smiled softly, her eyes creasing even more. She was a sun worshipper, always had been. I remembered watching her lie out in the sunshine, slowly baking, at the Okaporo colony. Back when she was my brood mother, and my parents were still alive, and my sister was nothing more special than I was. Destined to become a trader, dealing in memories people

1

wanted to offload. Narata had seemed impossibly old to me even then.

I grunted in reply, knowing that I didn't need to offer anything more. She knew why I always wore it loose, always shrouding my face. While she was happy to parade the three scars that crossed her right eye, the scars that marked her out as a trader, I preferred to cover mine. Not that my scars were the only way to know what I was; my hair, the colour of my skin, the shape of my nose. Everything about me was pure trader. I couldn't possibly be anything else.

And while Narata seemed to be oblivious to any of the side-glances or outright stares we attracted, I felt every single one as if it were a finger poked into my chest.

I took another sip from my drink. It was some kind of iced fruit thing, but it boasted a lot more watery, tasteless ice than actual fruit juice. Still, it was cold, and that was all that mattered.

Next to me, Dai stretched his arms up behind his head, revealing two dark patches of sweat on his shirt, his body exhaling a stifling whiff of it. He was one of those men that always looked tanned, even in the winter, the muddy colour of it catching in his wrinkles.

"You shouldn't suffer," he said to me. "No one would care about your scars in this part of the city. It's crawling with traders."

"Maybe I just don't want anyone seeing me with a rogue," I replied. "We are supposed to be mortal enemies, after all."

He squinted at me. "Well, I hate you. Despise you, in fact. There. Good enough?" He smiled and winked. I resisted the urge to punch him.

I looked up as Malia and Firefinch came out of the diner. Dai stuck his foot out and Firefinch tripped on it, somehow managing to keep hold of the drinks he carried. He aimed a kick back at Dai but missed him by quite a way. This was how the rogues were together, always throwing punches and insults. It passed for some kind of affection.

They settled themselves at another table, heads together, oblivious to the rest of the world.

Dai gestured towards them, a limp chip dangling from his fingers, a glob of ketchup threatening to drip from the end of it.

"What's that mumbo-jumbo they're speaking?" he asked. "They've been yabbering away like that for weeks."

"They're speaking Arukumbi," I replied.

"People still know how to speak that?"

"Apparently so. Malia's been teaching Firefinch. He's picking it up pretty quickly, too."

"What's the point?" The chip in his hand finally made its way into his mouth. "Why does he need to know some dead language from some forgotten culture that doesn't even have anything to do with him?"

I smiled. "Look at him. Those pale blue eyes. You don't think he might just have some Arukumbi in him? Besides, their culture is far from being forgotten, and their language is clearly very much alive. Just because you aren't part of something yourself, it doesn't mean it doesn't exist."

Dai shrugged. "Rogues don't obsess over the past. It's pointless. That's a pursuit for the likes of traders and, apparently, Arukumbi."

"Perhaps if rogues actually had some kind of history they would be interested in it. If they didn't just spring up from getting up one morning and feeling a bit pissed off with the world." I heard Narata choke on a laugh.

"And perhaps," replied Dai, "if you traders weren't so wrapped up in your own sense of self pity, because what else do you have to do with your day, you might be able to learn something about rogues."

"Well, perhaps—"

"Enough," said Narata, cutting me off. "You're acting like children bickering like that."

"We weren't bickering," Dai said. "We were merely expressing an interest in one another's cultures." He flashed me a grin. He never took anything seriously, not even an argument.

"Either way," continued Narata, "we didn't come all the way to Nagamoto to sit around chatting outside greasy dives like this. Maybe we should focus on why we're actually here."

"You mean we didn't come for the gourmet food?" Dai smiled again, his mouth full of half-chewed potato. He nodded and swallowed his food down. "You're right. Let's see what the latest is."

He lifted his hands up in front of him and drew out a box with his forefingers and thumbs. A lit screen hovered in the air before us, quickly loading with information. The tiny implants under his skin allowed him to scroll through the on-screen text.

If I tried to touch it, my finger would simply pass right through. I couldn't feel or interact with such screens, not without implants. And I wasn't about to let anyone inject microchips into me. Who knew what information they transmitted?

"Here we go," said Dai, finally ceasing the dizzying stream of information.

He'd stopped on a news article. We all knew what it said, it was the reason we were here.

"Doesn't look like they've updated anything else, other than a whole load of speculation. It's what we already knew: the Nagamoto alderman died unexpectedly last night at his home. Suspected heart attack."

"So, what now?" I asked.

"Luckily for us, I know someone on the security team that cover all the government officials. He's already briefed me about a few things they're not saying in the papers. Apparently, two intruder alarms were set off that night. One was tripped on one of the exterior doors, and another from the bedroom. That one was a panic button, one that the alderman had to physically press himself. I don't know about you, but I suspect there may have been someone else in that house last night. Someone who wasn't supposed to be there."

"Does he know any more than that?"

"He wasn't posted on that specific detail, so he didn't know anything more when I spoke to him earlier. But I'm meeting him in ten minutes or so, and hopefully he'll have found out a little bit more."

As he got up, Dai shoved another handful of chips into his mouth, ketchup coating his fingers.

"Look after the lovebirds," he said to Narata, gesturing towards Malia and Firefinch. He looked at me. "Are you coming?"

I jumped to my feet, glad to leave the smell of greasy burgers behind me.

2

KIOTO

The security buildings were located in the city centre, surrounded by a battalion of shining pillars of offices. The towers seemed to reach all the way to the clouds, and I marvelled at how monumental it was, and how tiny it made me feel. Once, people had built structures like this for the love of their faith, but these stood as a testament of how much the modern world loved enterprise, and wealth. That was the faith they draped around themselves, a saccharine display with no hint of subtlety.

"Close your mouth," hissed Dai. "You look like a tourist."

I jabbed him with my elbow. "How is it that you always manage to have some kind of friend, or contact, or someone who owes you a favour exactly when we need one? It all seems a little bit convenient."

Dai laughed and nudged me back. "If it was that convenient, he'd be head of security here. This guy's just a nobody with a uniform. Most of his job involves fishing dead rodents out of the swimming pools of rich clients. I'm not certain he's going to be of any use to us at all."

"And he's running late."

Dai nodded. "Yes, he's running late."

The street was packed with people in suits hurrying past, the creases in their trousers as sharp as blades. They hurried into buildings, hurried out of buildings, hurried across the road, called impatient greetings to other people who were equally hurried. They had no time to stare at a trader and a rogue. I couldn't imagine living like that, keeping that kind of pace all the time. And every single one of them walked with a screen floating along with them, chattering away, or scrolling, scrolling, scrolling.

"How do they walk around so distracted all the time?" I asked Dai, gesturing around me. "Aren't people always bumping into each other?"

He laughed. "You're joking, right?"

I shook my head. "No."

He laughed again.

"Can't you just call this friend of yours?" I sighed. The impatience here was contagious.

"He's ridiculously paranoid. I think he fancies himself as a spy from some movie. It's all clandestine meetings and secret notes. He won't let me call him because he says anyone could be listening. Just be patient."

It was hard to feel patient in the kaleidoscope of urgency that spun around us. But, finally, Dai straightened, and said "Here he comes."

The man that approached really was a nobody in a uniform. Middling height, thick around the middle, receding hair, doughy features. There was nothing striking about him, even his demeanour encouraged you to look right past him. I wondered how many times he'd watched others promoted ahead of him.

"Sorry I'm late." The loose skin under his chin swung back and forth as he shook his head. "The office is in complete chaos. Despite the security crackdown after what happened last night, there's been another incident this morning. There was an attempt on a reader's life too. It's a bad day to be in government."

"Is the reader alright?" Dai asked. His tone held no note of concern, it was more like excitement. He was such a vulture.

"Completely unharmed, luckily. But, as you can imagine, it's shaken everyone up."

Only then did the man register me. He frowned, his bushy eyebrows lowering like curtains over his eyes. "Who's this?" He looked back at Dai as he asked the question, not a thought to ask me directly.

Dai grinned. "She's my prisoner."

The man looked back at me, his frown deepening. He reached up a set of stubby fingers and pushed my hair back, revealing my scar. He snatched his hand away as if I had tried to bite it. I wished that I had.

"She's a trader," he hissed.

"I guess so," Dai replied.

"I can't believe you brought a trader here. You realise we're stood outside the top security office in the country. And you bring a trader here?" He glanced around. "Someone might have already seen me with her. How can you be so stupid?" He pushed Dai towards the edge of the pavement. "Come on, come on, move."

Hurrying on ahead of us, the man crossed the road, barely even looking for traffic before stepping out. The vehicles stopped automatically for pedestrians, their sensors ticking. The technology advances in auto cars had suppressed their own authority on the road.

He beckoned us up a side alley that smelt of vinegar and urine.

"I can't believe you, Dai," he said, jabbing his finger into the rogue's chest. "Bringing a trader here, on today of all days."

"What's special about today?" asked Dai.

The guy rolled his eyes. "Really? I thought you kept on top of things. There's another anti-trader rally. Ever since that lot," he gestured wildly towards me, "started killing off government officials, these rallies have become more and more frequent. They're well organised, and huge. Thousands, tens of thousands of people out demanding action."

"Traders have nothing to do with the deaths," I

muttered, but I knew it was futile. No one wanted to listen to someone they saw as the enemy. And we'd always been that. This was just an excuse to hate us even more.

He continued as if I hadn't even spoken. "They're calling for the instant deaths of all traders. Can you imagine what it's like trying to control that? And then there's always traders with a death wish who turn up to counter protest. It's a nightmare. We're trying to keep the truth about the alderman under wraps because, if that lot knew what really happened, there'd be a full-scale riot."

"What did happen?" Dai asked.

He didn't even pay heed to Dai speaking. I smiled; it wasn't personal after all. The man just loved the sound of his own voice. "But you know what journalists are like. They're like sharks as soon as they smell blood, or even the potential for blood. And it's not just the professional ones, these days you have anyone with a blog or a vlog or whatever they call them turning up to make videos and take selfies. The bedroom journalists are even worse. Bloody wannabes."

"What really happened to the alderman?" Dai asked again.

"Oh, yeah. Well, we still don't have a definite cause of death, we'll have to wait for the official medical reports, but according to the guys who have been out to the house, it definitely wasn't a heart attack. Because, according to them, that house is absolutely drenched in blood."

3

KIOTO

We watched as Dai's contact hurried back to the security offices, crossing the road again without a glance in either direction.

Dai laid his hand on my shoulder. "We'd better get you out of here, the last thing we need is to bump into a load of blood-thirsty protesters."

I nodded. I wasn't about to become a trader with a death wish.

"We'd better avoid the main streets," Dai said, leading me further into the alleyway.

"I hope you're not going to get us lost."

"Never. Rogues have an excellent sense of direction." He looked back at me and grinned. "Even if we don't have a history of our own."

"You better be right," I said, stepping over a

rotting half-eaten baguette. "I've heard stories about the giant rats in the cities."

Dai stopped ahead of me. For a moment I wondered if the stories about the rats might actually be true. I imagined its teeth, curving from its jaw, mashing, yellow, saliva dripping from them as it weighed up the meat on our bones.

"What is it?" I whispered.

He stepped aside and gestured for me to come up next to him. He pointed.

We were standing at a crossroads in the grid of back streets, and to our left, the narrow avenue led down to the main street, giving us a clear view of the rally passing by.

There was something beautiful about it; celebratory, carnivalesque. Bright colours, streamers, flags, drums, trumpets. But then there were the placards, and the chanting, which seemed so at odds with the festival appearance. They called for the execution of all traders, instantly, and without mercy. Beheadings, hangings, firing squads, they all had their own ideas, but the goal was universal. The party atmosphere made it eerily grotesque. I backed away.

Dai turned me around and pushed me in the opposite direction.

"How can that be legal?" I asked, not even really looking for an answer. "They're asking for genocide. They're inciting murder. How can they be allowed to do that?"

Dai shrugged. "Sign of the times, I guess."

A man stepped into the street ahead of us and

I stopped. He was carrying a thick rope circled into a noose. He also stopped, backed up a couple of steps, and stared.

"Trader scum," he said. "You should be dead."

My heart hammered and I shuffled back, almost tripping over Dai's boots.

Dai stepped around me. "Move on," he said. He placed his hands on his hips, displaying the guns holstered on his belt.

The protester gave me another hard stare before scurrying away.

Once we were clear of the city centre, Dai stopped and scratched his head, another waft of sweat escaping.

"I need a drink," he said.

"What's the plan now?" I asked.

He smiled at me. "Aren't you ever off duty?"

"I'd just like to get business over and done with so that I can get back to my sister."

Dai looked around. We'd wandered into the suburbs and, where we were standing, there wasn't so much as a convenience store.

"Business it is then. We should head over to the alderman's house, see what we can find out."

I shook my head. "We won't get within a mile of that place, you heard what your friend said, they're fighting off journalists over there. Unless you have a conveniently placed friend with a bit more influence? And you really think turning up with a trader in tow is a good idea? I'll be lynched."

"You're right." Dai nodded thoughtfully. "Maybe we'll have better luck following up on the attempted murder of the reader. He's still alive so there's less of a story there, especially with the alderman dead."

"Do you think they were both done by the same vessel?"

"It's likely. We rarely find more than one vessel in a city at any one time. Mind you, we've never had a vessel attempt two murders in such quick succession before. If only your sister was proving a little more useful."

"You saw her, she's in agony. She started getting a headache before we even reached Nagamoto, and it wasn't long before it became a full-blown migraine."

"Our previous vessel never reacted like that."

"You can't expect her to work when she can't even see straight. You know the vessels can't get too close to each other without some kind of reaction."

"But this severe?" He sighed. "Maybe Omori needs more training, or better training."

"Remember that Narata's never trained a vessel before. Even for a brood mother, it's not exactly familiar territory. We're all just feeling our way through it."

"Then maybe Omori's not a strong enough vessel."

"Maybe she's too strong," I argued. "Or maybe all vessels are getting stronger, did you think of that?"

Dai held up his hands defensively. "Alright, alright, maybe you're right. I apologise for insulting your family honour." He turned away, adding "or whatever" under his breath.

I swallowed back my next sentence.

"Why don't you give her a call?" he said. "See how she's doing. At the very least she can use her magic vessel connection to tell us whether the other vessel's already left the city or not."

4

KIOTO

I sat on the edge of the bed and stroked Omori's hair. She opened one eye, just a crack, and squinted up at me.

"How're you feeling?" I asked.

She groaned, and closed her eye again.

"At least the vessel's left the city, so you can start to get better. Just concentrate on that for now."

"And when I do get better," Omori croaked, "we'll be off chasing another vessel, and all the pain comes back again. What if Dai decides I'm completely useless and he's better off just killing me?"

I squeezed her hand. "I'm not going to let that happen. Get some rest, and eat something. Malia made you a whole tray of food, so try to get something down. I'll go and speak to Narata."

I found Narata in the small kitchen downstairs. We were staying in one of the apparently many houses Dai owned, or, at least, had access to, but this one was far smaller than his main residence in Kumonayo.

"Out," I said, and the few rogues that were gathered there disappeared.

"What's going on?" I asked Narata. "When are we leaving? Don't you think we've bided our time enough already?"

"I know you're frustrated—" Narata began.

I cut her off. "Omori can't do this anymore. And if she doesn't find a way to work through it, Dai will kill her. We can't just wait around like sitting ducks."

"I just think that now's not the time."

"What are you waiting for? The perfect weather? The moon to be aligned?"

"I've been reading about some new strategies with Omori. I'd like to give them a go."

"How about we give them a go in the safety of a colony?"

"Do you really think Dai won't come looking for us? I need to get him on side. I think that negotiation is our most powerful tool right now, for everyone's sake."

I eyed her closely. "Or maybe you have no intention of leaving."

"Of course I do." She turned away.

"You never wanted to escape, did you? You never wanted to rebuild Okaporo. You just said that to get me onboard. You lied to me."

"Kioto, I don't want anyone to die, especially not my own people, and I carry the lives of every vessel we've killed in my heart like a stone."

"You carry them? How do you think Omori feels? Dai's using her connection to other vessels to find them."

"I'm sorry about that, but... it's unavoidable."

"It's perfectly avoidable," I snapped. "We leave, and we'll be avoiding it all."

"You can't just run away from what's happening."

I looked at her for a moment. "What exactly is happening?"

"You've seen what the vessels are doing, how dangerous they are. This is treason, Kioto, they're starting a war. And you've seen the effect on Omori; they're getting stronger. They're not going to stop. How long do you think people are going to be content with protests? They'll be rioting soon, while the government are too scared or too stupid to do anything. They have an enemy they can't see, one they can't even hope to understand, and they're certainly not going to ask us for help. But the people see us. They see this." She pointed to the scars over her eyes. "And it's not going to matter whether we're vessels or not, they don't see any distinction. They'll be dragging traders out of the colonies and stringing them up themselves."

"They've deployed armed security to the colonies."

Narata sighed. "How loyal do you suppose

they'll be to the traders? They're grudgingly doing this. It's more an exercise in government PR than actually giving any kind of protection to the colonies."

"If the vessels are getting stronger you need to train Omori better. You've left her vulnerable with your half-hearted attempts."

"Yes, Kioto, I don't know what I'm doing." She threw her hands into the air. "Is that what you want to hear? I'm trawling through books written decades ago, and it takes time, and not everything works. I can't ask for help because we have no idea who we can trust. I've been betrayed too, Kioto. You act like you're so hard done by, like you're the only one who's been hurt." She stepped closer and lowered her voice. "I trusted Tokai. I trusted her with the most precious thing Okaporo had. She betrayed me. She betrayed all of us, and I blame myself every day for that. Stop acting like a spoilt child. This is so much bigger than you. Bigger than Omori, bigger than Okaporo. When are you going to see that?"

I stared at the tiled floor.

"Something unprecedented is happening," continued Narata. "We've never faced an enemy like this before. We need to see this through."

"See it through to what? The day they're done with Omori, and they kill her too? Finish the job?"

Narata grabbed my hands and held them tightly. "I will not let that happen. I'll never let that happen, I promise."

I grunted. Her promises didn't seem to mean

very much.

"We will return to Okaporo, we will rebuild it. But we can't do that now. We need to see this through, we need to wait until it's safe for us. Not while the world is like this."

"Like what?"

"Divided. Dangerous and divided."

5

KIOTO

I swept out of the kitchen and straight into the common room. Bodies lounged everywhere here: they were draped over furniture, stretched out on the floor, leant against walls and door frames. A large TV dominated the far wall, some kind of car chase computer game played at dizzying speeds, and everyone was focussed on it. Well, except for two people.

I prodded Malia. "I need to speak to you."

She barely lifted her head. "Yeah, yeah, later."

"Now." I lifted one of Firefinch's legs off her. You could barely tell where one of them ended and the other began. They were tangled together like brambles.

Malia groaned and lolled her head. "Really?"

"Come on."

She grunted and lifted herself off the sofa, picking her feet out from between Firefinch's limbs. I led her into the corridor outside.

"You know what all of this is doing to Omori," I whispered to her, "so I just spoke to Narata about us leaving, about our plans to escape, and she has no intention of doing it. I don't think she ever did. She actually agrees with Dai. She wants to see all the vessels dead. She says she won't let him kill Omori, but if we don't escape, that's what's going to happen. She says we have to 'see this through', whatever that's supposed to mean."

Malia closed her eyes for a moment, as if bracing herself for her reply. "Narata's probably right. You've seen what's happening, how Lobaya is right now. At the moment, we're actually doing something. If you leave, you leave the world to descend even further into the pit it's already slipping into."

"Is it so bad to want to save my sister's life? To want to rebuild our home?"

"Of course not, but there are bigger things right now. It's not all about what you want. For once, Kioto, you need to think of other people."

"I'm thinking of Omori," I snapped.

"Are you? Were you thinking of her when you dragged her into all this in Kumonayo? Or were you thinking about your desire to have at least a part of your family back? Are you thinking about her with your need to rebuild Okaporo? A place she barely even remembers and feels no connection to? And me, you want to drag me there too. I served my purpose, you got your sister's memories restored to her. What am I even still doing here? Do I not get a say either?"

"I'm sorry, I guess saving everyone's life got in the way of me thinking straight."

"You're not saving mine."

"I did."

She cocked her head. "Actually, Omori did. But I'm not in any danger now. I actually like being here."

I threw my hands up. "Then whatever, stay, become a rogue."

Malia placed her hand on my arm. "Is it really such a bad thing to be? Come on, we've been with them for almost three years now, we've tracked down and killed a small handful of vessels, but what else? Have they done anything else?"

"They're holding a gun to my sister's head."

Malia dropped her hand. "Look, Kioto, at the end of the day, you'll either do something, or you won't. If you're going to do something, then go do it, stop talking about it, and if you're not going to do anything, then stop whining."

I opened my mouth and then clamped it shut. I'd never heard Malia speak to anyone in this way before.

"Since the day I was born," she continued, "I've been owned by someone, being told where to go and what to do. Having memories pushed into me and dragged out of me. I had no say in any of it. First, I was owned by a series of merchants, and now I'm owned by Dai. For a while, I was owned by you."

"I freed you. I never owned you."

She raised an eyebrow. "I was told where to go and what to do. That's not any kind of freedom. But there was one choice that I did have. One choice that could never be taken away from me. I could either make the most of my situation, or I could let it become so unbearable that all I wanted was to die. Even as a smudger I found moments of happiness. The carriers rallied together, it was like a family to me. And we even managed to make our own fun. We made the most of it. And that's what I'm doing now. I've finally got a friend, a boy I might actually like, a boy who might actually like me back. A little piece of normality, something other people get, that I never imagined could be mine. And, you know what? I don't know how it's all going to turn out, I don't know what might happen in the future, but I'm having fun finding out. You have a choice, Kioto. Stop playing the victim. Make the most of what you have, or do something to change it. Just stop talking big when you don't back it up with action. Try actually becoming the person you always pretend to be."

6

KIOTO

As I kicked the door open, it swung back and bounced on its hinges. I shot my hand up to stop it from slamming back into me. I cursed myself for messing up the entrance I'd planned in my head. Everything was going wrong. I was still reeling from Malia's tirade. Mostly because it had rung true. So here I was, taking action before I talked myself out of it.

I looked straight at Dai and marched towards his desk. He fancied himself as some kind of general of a great army, stood, leaning over the workspace, both hands braced against its surface. A number of screens glowed, lighting his face in a sickly hue.

He glanced up and held a finger up to me,

gesturing for me to wait.

"Sorry about that," he said to one of the screens. "Carry on."

"There's not much else to say, really." An electronic voice crackled back at him. "But I would really appreciate your input on this. It's way above my own expertise, and I'm floundering, if I'm honest. So, can you come?"

"Let me get back to you, but it definitely sounds like something worth pursuing." He touched the screen and it disappeared. He straightened up and looked at me. "You must have something important to say after such a dramatic entrance."

The fire in my stomach had begun to fizzle out, so I took a deep breath and tried to reignite the flames.

"We're leaving. Me. Omori. We're going to walk out of here, and you're not going to stop us."

Dai looked at me for a moment and then sat down. "I've just spoken to a friend of mine who works the border patrol up at Aojima, that's the call you interrupted with your door slamming."

"Did you hear me?" I asked. The fire wavered again.

"Yes, I did. So, up at the border, they've had a number of traders coming in from Qathab."

"Dai. Did you hear me? I said we're leaving."

He sighed. "Kioto, if you were actually going to leave, you'd have just upped and done it. You wouldn't have come in here to ask my permission first."

"I'm not asking your permission."

"Then what are you doing? You're so keen on talking about doing big things, that you seem to forget to actually do them. We both know you're not going to walk out of here. Look, Kioto, I like having you on board with this. I trust you, believe it or not. You're sensible and considered, most of the time, and your lack of trust in practically everyone you ever come across is a useful trait. I think we work pretty well together. I also think that you quite enjoy it. Look, let me tell you what my friend at the border said. There's been an increasing influx of groups of traders coming into Lobaya from Qathab. Do you know where that is?"

I rolled my eyes. "Of course. I'm not completely uneducated."

"Well, he's pretty sure that a good number of them have been vessels. More and more so, in fact. I think it's worth checking out."

"Maybe that's why Omori's reactions to the vessels have been getting worse. Perhaps because these vessels are different. Or stronger. If they're stronger than Lobayan vessels, though, I don't know what we're going to do about them. We need to get to the border to see this for ourselves."

The fire in my stomach had extinguished itself, but it had been replaced by another. This was too important to abandon. These vessels put Omori in danger. They put all of us in danger.

"Right, then I guess it's another road trip, to Aojima. We'll take Omori, of course, so that she can confirm the presence of vessels and if it is the Qathab vessels causing such an extreme reaction in her."

"No. It's too much for her. She's not coping. I'm not going to walk her into a situation just to see how much we can make her suffer."

Dai shrugged. "This was your theory, Kioto. How are we going to test it out otherwise? We need to take her towards vessels that we know are from Qathab."

"Fine. But she gets nowhere near them. We'll keep her at a safe distance."

Dai nodded. "You're the boss." He smiled.

7

KIOTO

I sat on the edge of Omori's bed. She was finally sitting upright, and finally eating. Malia fussed around her, offering her more food and all manner of drinks choices.

"So we're going to Aojima to check out what's happening at the border."

"And what about me?" asked Omori. "You're going to use my head as a test to find out how strong these vessels are?"

"Of course not, I wouldn't put you in that kind of danger. You'll be at a safe distance, and you can choose where. You're in control, ok?"

Malia tugged on my arm, turning me towards her. "If these vessels are as strong as you think they might be," she said, "is it even safe for you to go? You have no protection against them, and we've seen what they can do, and what they're willing to do. Five minutes ago you were talking about escaping, and now you're walking right towards the lion's den."

"You said Narata was right," I reminded her. "You said that we needed to see this through."

"But, like this?" asked Omori. "What if... seriously, what if my head actually explodes?"

"Like I said, you go as close as you feel safe. No one's going to argue with you. I wouldn't put you in unnecessary danger."

"Will Narata be with me?"

"Of course."

Malia set about tidying away dishes. She crashed plates together, rattled cutlery, sloshed water. "I think you're crazy," she said to me. "And you're even crazier for going along with it," she said to Omori. "Think about what you're doing. This whole thing has escalated very suddenly into something way more dangerous than it was. For all of us. For all of Lobaya. You're trying to catch a shadow, and you don't even know who's casting it."

8

KIOTO

Aojima was the largest city in Lobaya, stretching out lazily from the border and on towards Naradai. It boasted the tallest building in Lobaya, and the largest park. It was the oldest Lobayan city; the first settlement after the Lobayans invaded the country. Of course, the Arukumbi settlements pre-dated Aojima by hundreds of years, but the city was the proud owner of a number of historical buildings, like the old courthouse, now a museum and fancy cafe, several art galleries, the police station, and the slave market.

Despite its gruesome purpose, the slave market was an undeniably impressive and beautiful building. It was a large, circular structure, set in the centre of oddly serene gardens. The exterior was ringed with pillars, each one deeply carved with the Lobayan coat of arms.

Lobayans had originally arrived in Arukumbi with their own slaves, but once they began enslaving the natives, they no longer had to make their own people suffer such a life. The building announced itself proudly, unashamed of its purpose and legacy, but as the citizens passed by, I noticed that they turned their eyes the other way. It was no wonder that the surrounding grounds were peaceful; no one wanted to spend their time there.

"It's a despicable practice," I muttered to Dai. "I can't believe we continue with it."

Dai shrugged. "As long as there's money in it, the lives of the Arukumbi will mean very little."

"Sometimes, I'm ashamed to be Lobayan."

Dai shivered. It was oddly cold in the shadow of such a building. "Let's get moving," he said. "We're here to work, not for sight-seeing."

The rogues in Aojima lived a little more like I expected rogues to. They weren't quite living in caves like I'd known some to do, but had taken over some disused warehouses at one edge of the city. The vast spaces were separated into makeshift rooms by screens, bookcases, shelving units, or by piles of boxes. A few children ignored the conventions and scrambled around on top of the improvised room dividers.

As we entered the building, Dai was warmly greeted, but the eyes that fell on myself, Omori, and Narata had a look I rarely saw. I was used to looks of hatred, disgust, or indifference, but I didn't often see that look of fear, especially from rogues. A few of them backed away from us, others watched us suspiciously, flinching if we raised an arm too quickly, or looked their way.

Dai and Narata quickly disappeared off for discussions and meetings the rest of us weren't invited to, and we were pointed towards some kind of recreation room.

The space quietened as we approached, and rogues shifted their eyes quickly from our faces to their screens.

We settled ourselves onto a threadbare sofa that had been vacated on our arrival.

"I don't get it," I grumbled. "Dai says he trusts me and values my input, and then he goes off into secret meetings. And we're put in the playpen with the other kids."

"If anyone should know what's happening, it should be me," said Omori.

"Stop whining," said Firefinch. "You may think you've been put in the playpen, but this is the best source of information there is. Rogue kids are very, very good at listening. We'll probably find out more in here than Dai will."

"Not if they're all scared of us," I whispered.

"Let me ask around, I'll find someone keen to talk."

Firefinch was back quickly with a jumpy young rogue he introduced to us as Besra. The boy couldn't have been any older than fourteen or so, and never stopped moving. He tapped his fingers against his jiggling knee, his eyes flicking back and forth between us all. He made me feel jumpy and nervous.

"So, you want to know about the vessels?" He spoke so quickly his words tripped over one another, as if the whole sentence were just a single expression.

"Yes," I said. "Tell us everything."

"We've been aware of traders coming in from Qathab for a long time, years. It's nothing unusual, not overly suspicious. But over the last year or so we became aware that some of them were vessels."

"How?" I asked. "How did you know?"

"We've got a couple of people who used to be traders who run with us. They noticed it first. They couldn't even put their finger on it. Just a feeling. Just something in their eyes, the way they looked at you. Our contacts at the border confirmed it. They'd been thinking the same thing. To start with, we were tracking them, following them, trying to kill them. But they weren't like the vessels we'd come across before. They were stronger, more powerful. Almost inhuman. They killed several of us before we stopped going after them."

"How were they killing the rogues?" I asked.

"Making them do stuff. Putting thoughts in their head."

"How did they do it?"

"They had to be touching them. But it's not like traders. They don't even need to touch their forehead. It's anything; hand, arm, leg, wherever they find bare skin. And it need only be for a second, and then the thought is there. One of the rogues shot four others, one of which was his own brother, and, like, blood brother, his actual real brother. He said the desire to kill popped into his head in just a second. From nowhere. He didn't even realise the vessel had touched him. He said the compulsion to kill the others was all he could think about. There was nothing else in his head. He had no choice. It took over his whole body, just this need to kill those other rogues."

"Is he here? Can we talk to him?"

Besra shook his head. "He couldn't live with what he'd done. We all told him it wasn't his fault, but he never stopped blaming himself. And the vessels are coming in more and more now, but always at pretty regular intervals. They never hang around in Aojima for long, and there's never more than two of them in the city at one time. When one moves on, another one comes across the border."

"Where do they go to?"

"All over, but they all head towards the coast eventually. Honporo seems to be their focus." He swallowed. "I've heard people describe them as 'weapons', and I'd agree with that. They'll kill anyone who stands in their way. Even traders."

9

KIOTO

I leaned my head back against the sofa and groaned. The few days we'd been here had dragged, and turned into an indistinguishable mush of stifling heat, take-out food, and iced fruit smoosh drinks. I'd never been so bored.

Omori patted me on the shoulder. "You ok?"

"Bored," I groaned, drawing the word out for almost as long as we'd been in Aojima.

"I have some good news for you."

I looked up at her.

"One of the vessels has just left the city."

I sat up and turned around to face her. "Seriously?"

She tapped her head. "Just gone."

I stood up. "Have you told Dai?"

"I told you first."

I grabbed hold of her hands and shook them both up and down. "Finally." I kissed her on the forehead. "Finally."

The border control wasn't far out of the city, just a short burst of scrubland between the last of Aojima's suburbs, and the small community that surrounded the border office. Many of the workers lived here with their families, and it had become a fully functioning town.

We were greeted by Dai's friend, Kanak. Dai was warmly greeted with a hug, I was greeted by a hesitant handshake.

"You can wait in the overnight quarters. There's a couple of beds, a TV, some vending machines. It's nothing fancy, but if one vessel's left Aojima, I doubt you'll have long to wait for another. You can almost set your watch by them."

The overnight quarters were small and unwelcoming. A fluorescent light flickered slightly overhead, and the vending machines hummed in unison.

I lay down on a bed and folded my arms behind my head.

"Do you want something?" Dai asked, gesturing towards the vending machines.

"As long as it's not coated in chocolate, or some sloppy iced fruit thing."

"You'll come to love them," he said, tossing me a packet of sandwiches.

"I just don't know why you people are so

averse to food that actually looks like food." I pulled back the plastic film on my sandwiches. "Or that actually smells like food."

Dai shrugged and perched himself on the other bed. "Convenience sells. And at a premium."

"I guess if you're too busy to actually enjoy your food, you really don't care what it tastes or looks like, huh?"

Dai grinned at me with a mouthful of sandwich. "Yummy."

"I've got my own lunch, thanks, I don't need to see yours as well."

"Why are you always so angry at the world? Is it just part of your bad-ass image, or is something genuinely upsetting you?"

"You're upsetting me," I quipped. And then I thought of Tian. When we'd first met, we'd spent some time in a room just like this, recovering from the throw after performing a memory extraction. Well, I'd been recovering, he'd been annoyingly chirpy. I'd thought of him constantly over the years, every time someone spoke like him, or moved like him, or I thought I caught the scent of him. He'd sacrificed his own safety to save mine and Malia's lives, led the rogues away from us, and I had no idea whether he was still alive or not. Three years without any word at all. There wasn't much hope.

"You'll grow to love me," Dai said.

"Just like that fruity ice mush?"

"Just like that."

We were interrupted by a gentle knock on the door. It slowly opened and Kanak's head appeared in the gap.

"We've got a group of traders from Qathab. Just arrived. You ready?"

I stood up and discarded my sandwiches into the bin. "Do you think there's a vessel with them?" I asked.

"Not seen them myself yet, but I wouldn't be surprised." He shuddered. "Something's just not right with them, with the way they look at you. It's like they know what you're thinking. Or, I suppose, they know what you're going to be thinking, once they've put the thoughts in your head." He cocked his head towards the door. "Come on, I'll show you where we're holding them."

He marched ahead of us, up a series of corridors, and I almost had to jog to keep up with him.

When he stopped, he opened the door into an uncomfortably familiar interview room. I'd been in one of these before, in the police station in Kumonayo. Four women sat on the far side of the small desk, and they turned towards us, as one, when we entered. They were more like a single creature than four distinct beings.

I looked back at them, my eyes resting on the vessel. I instantly knew. I didn't know how I knew, but I did. And I couldn't shake the feeling that she knew that I knew.

Kanak sat opposite the women. He pulled a screen up in front of him and made a show of checking it. He cleared his throat.

"What is your reason for entering Lobaya

today?"

"Tourism," one of the traders replied.

"Where do you plan to visit while you are in Lobaya?"

"We'd like to see the ocean. Qathab is a land-locked country."

"You've travelled to Lobaya passing through Merhan which has a coast of its own. Why travel all the way to Lobaya when you could see the ocean in Merhan?"

"Merhan's coastline is nothing but cliffs. We've heard stories of the beautiful sandy beaches here." She smiled at her companions. "We'd like to work on our tans."

"Other than the beaches, what else do you hope to see?"

The trader grinned coldly. "We would like to see the beautiful government buildings in Honporo. We hear they're very old and impressive."

"Anything else you hope to see while you're here?"

"We'd like to see the slave market here in Aojima. Explore the history of the Lobayan culture." Her eyes flicked up to mine for a second.

"Do you have any intentions to work while you are in Lobaya?"

"No. We are just tourists."

"Do you have accommodation booked for your stay?"

"We'll be staying at the trader colonies."

"Do you have any documentation to show that agreement? Any letters or messages from the brood mothers?"

"It was all verbally agreed."

Kanak leaned back in his chair. "Of course it was."

"You have no right to be holding us. Our papers are in order, and we have no requirement to prove residence to you. And they have no right to be here, either." She nodded towards myself and Dai.

"They are here as consultants, and they have every right to be here."

"She's a government consultant? A trader?" She spat onto the floor. "I know what your government thinks of traders here. This interview is over."

My eyes flicked to the vessel, and hers were focussed deeply on Kanak. I could feel her determination, her intent. I could feel that she would do whatever it took to get out of this room, even if it meant someone had to die.

"This interview is over when I say it's over," Kanak replied.

I wanted to place my hand on his shoulder, warn him somehow, get him to back off, but the traders would see, and they'd guess why I was so cautious. They'd guess that I could see their vessel's thoughts.

"What is she doing in here?" the trader demanded again. "And him," she looked directly at Dai, "He is what you call a 'rogue', is he not? A killer of traders. What's he doing here?"

"They are here as consultants. The

government employs all kinds of people for their expertise, and that is no business of yours."

"Rogues and traders?" She folded her arms across her chest and looked at the vessel. "We're not going to say anything else."

The vessel stood up. "In fact, we're leaving."

"Sit down," Kanak ordered.

"You have no rights to stop us."

Kanak stood up, his hand on the gun holstered at his hip. "Sit down now."

The vessel's gaze didn't waver from Kanak's face, but her mind reached out to his gun, and I could see it. My feet were stuck, solid, to the floor, my arms cemented at my sides, my gaze fixed, unwavering, on the vessel. I couldn't move. I couldn't stop this.

The other traders stood up, and Kanak placed himself between them and the door.

"Sit down, or I will use force." His fingers flickered against the grip of his gun.

"Kanak, no," I said.

"Sit down now!"

One of the traders spat at him, a shimmering globule of saliva landing on the side of his nose.

He pulled the gun free and pointed it at the traders. "I am authorised to shoot, now sit down."

"Kanak, put the gun away," I cried.

"Sit down!"

"Kanak!"

I wrenched my legs free from their immovability, and stumbled towards him. As I did, the vessel pushed past the other traders and reached out to him as well. She touched his hand, just for a moment.

"No!" I shouted.

Kanak swung around, focussing his gun on Dai. His eyes were blank, glazed, unfocussed. He was a puppet now.

"Kanak," said Dai. "Kanak, stop."

The vessel looked at me. "We will have free passage into Lobaya. You will not stop us entering the country. No one will. And you will not track us."

"No," Dai said. "Shoot me if you want, but you are not leaving this room."

"Dai, no," I said.

"We'll shoot everyone if we have to," the vessel replied. "We will enter Lobaya."

"Just let them go, Dai."

"No. We will not give in to terrorism."

"And you're prepared to be a martyr for that cause? What use are you if you're dead? Let them go, Dai."

"I won't be bullied—"

"What choice do you have? Let them go."

Dai grunted, his chest crumpling with defeat. "Fine. No one will stop you."

"Walk us out of here," the vessel said.

Dai nodded.

"And if you try to signal to anyone, I'll put a nasty little compulsion into your head too."

10

KIOTO

Kanak hadn't lifted his head out of his hands since they'd got him down to the overnight quarters, and all he'd said was how sorry he was, over and over.

Dai sat next to him and rubbed his back. "How many times do I have to tell you? That was not your fault. It was mind control, you couldn't have possibly done anything to stop it."

"I should have read the signs. I should have known what would happen."

"This is not your fault," Dai repeated.

Kanak finally raised his head, his eyes dark and bloodshot. "I'm trained in this, to read people. I should have known." He looked up at me. "You tried to warn me, but I just saw red. I wasn't thinking straight even before she touched me. And that's on me. That was all me."

I chewed my lip. "Perhaps not."

"How can we possibly defend our country against these people?" Kanak asked. "I've never, ever felt so powerless before. I'm a border guard, we're protecting the border of this country. Lobaya can't afford for us to be so powerless."

"Maybe there's something I can do," I said. "It's not much, and it's certainly not going to offer full protection, but it might slow them down a bit. I could teach you some mind blocking techniques. If you practice, you can become quite strong. The brain is like any other muscle in the body. At the very least, we'll be trying to do something rather than just giving in to them."

"Could you teach the other guards too?"

I nodded. "It could help a little, at least."

There was a sharp knock at the door and another guard stepped into the room. He looked at Kanak.

"I know this is the last thing you need right now, but there's a reader here, from Aojima. Come for an update on the situation. He wants to speak to you as the most senior guard here today. I'm sorry, but he refuses to speak to anyone else."

Kanak sighed. "Bloody government officials." He nodded. "Can you stall him for a bit? I just need to gather myself together."

"No problem." The guard disappeared, gently shutting the door behind him.

Kanak groaned. "This is the last thing I need. The readers show up here every once in a while for an official update. It's a pain. We give them feedback, numbers. And then we ask for help, for some kind of solution. And they say they'll get back to us. They never do. There's no government policy. No actions, no instructions, no sanctions. We need to be shutting down the border to these people, but the government are doing nothing."

"They're scared," I said.

"Too right, they're scared. And from what happened today, they're right to be. But a government can't act like that." He shook his head. "They won't risk war. Not against an enemy we can't defend against." He looked up at me. "Until now."

I held up my hands. "What I'm proposing is no kind of defence."

"It's more a defence than we have now."

"Are you going to tell the reader what happened today?" Dai asked.

Kanak nodded. "I have to. The government need to know just how dangerous these vessels are."

"Then you'll have to tell him about us," I muttered.

Kanak's face lit up with an idea. "I'll get him to come and talk to you, about your plan." He stood up. "Maybe you could actually be a government consultant."

He marched out of the room and I grimaced at Dai.

"What are we getting ourselves into?" I asked.

Dai smiled. "Hey, this is all on you. This was

your bright idea. I have no intentions of getting myself put on the government payroll." He shuddered. "Far too much responsibility."

"Too much expectation."

"Right. This idea of yours, do you think it will have any effect at all, this mind blocking?"

I shook my head. "Probably not. Well, not beyond giving the guards some extra confidence. Confidence can go a long way."

"It can also make you foolish."

"Thanks for the positivity."

Dai raised his eyebrows. "Misplaced confidence can get a person killed."

"Stop it."

"And you saw how chirpy Kanak was over it all."

"Stop it."

"That's a lot to have on your conscience."

I dropped down onto the other bed. "If we're talking about heavy consciences, you better check your own, rogue."

Dai smiled casually. It was annoying. "My conscience is clear," he said.

It was well over an hour before Kanak came back, creeping his head sheepishly around the door.

"Sorry that took so long, I've had to go over every detail about a hundred times with him. Now, it wasn't easy, believe me, but he's agreed to speak with you both. Come on."

I pushed myself to my feet. "Oh, I do believe you," I muttered.

We met the reader in a large meeting room, far different to the interview rooms. It was bright, with a line of floor to ceiling windows along one wall. Outside, dusk lit the trees in a gold light that flooded the room. I was relieved, and took in a deep breath. It felt like I'd spent the whole day shut up in small, cramped, windowless rooms.

"This is the trader I told you about," said Kanak. "This is Kioto."

"The government doesn't usually give audience to traders," the reader said to Kanak. He hadn't even looked at me once.

"We appreciate it," Kanak said. "If the guards here feel like they have even a little bit of protection against these vessels from Qathab, it will help them a lot. They're scared, and you can't control a border with fear."

"Traders," the reader said. "They need protection from the traders in Qathab. All of them. They're all the same, invading people's heads."

"Vessels and traders aren't the same at all," I said.

"They come from the same lines, the same families." Still, the reader spoke to Kanak, refusing to look in my direction.

"Yes, but they're very different. What I'm proposing is—"

"Officer Kanak told me what you're proposing." His eyes finally snapped onto me. "I can't give a trader permission to poke around in the heads of government employees. I can't trust where you might stick your grubby little mind control fingers."

"I don't control minds, I don't have that ability. I wouldn't be poking around in anyone's head. It's just teaching some techniques to block their thoughts."

"So you'd be able to teach them this without even touching them, yes?"

"Well, I'd need to check that they're doing it correctly, check the strength of their blocks."

"Aha, there you go. Prodding around in their brains."

"No, I—"

"Absolutely not." The reader stood up and turned back to Kanak. "The government will protect you, not colony rats."

"But the government aren't doing anything," Kanak replied.

"Diplomacy takes time. We need to do things properly. Not hand our minds over to the likes of her." He pointed at me.

"But while you're working on your diplomacy, we're defenceless. I could have killed Dai today."

"But you didn't." The reader turned to Dai. "Luckily for us. The rogue, Dai. I've heard of your reputation, and the Aojima seat is very impressed. We'd like you to remain here at the border to assess things for us." He looked at Kanak. "Here's the defence you're so desperate for." He turned back to Dai. "You'll be issued with a weapon, authority to fire it, and a generous pay offer."

Dai shook his head. "Actually, I was thinking of crossing over into Qathab. Sussing things out."

The reader nodded. "Then all of your expenses

will be paid, with extra compensation for your time."

Dai snorted. "Keep your money. I'm doing this because it's what I believe in, not because I want some kind of hero's homecoming parade. I'd rather not be on your payroll, thank you."

11

KIOTO

When we pulled up at the Aojima rogue camp, I barely managed to get out of the car before Omori threw herself into my arms. She hugged me tightly, her shoulder rammed into my throat. I prised her off before she suffocated me.

"What's going on?" I asked her.

"I thought you were dead," she said, her eyes streaming with tears.

"I'm fine, I'm fine." I pulled her back into my arms.

"I saw the gun, Kioto, I thought you were dead."

I pushed her away and held her at arm's length. "What? How did you see the gun?"

She rubbed at her eyes. "I've been working

with Narata on some new ways to control the headaches when I'm near other vessels. It's not got rid of them entirely, but they're so much better. I can still focus, still see. I followed the line of the pain today, reached out towards the vessel's mind. I saw the gun, I saw what she intended to do. I saw her place the thought into that guard. But while I could see her, she could also see me. She spoke to me, right inside my head, like it was actually me thinking the words. She said "Get out, or they all die." I was so scared, I was so scared that she'd killed you and it was my fault."

Omori dropped back into my arms again, her body limp. I rubbed her back.

"It's ok, I'm fine. But I don't want you doing that again, ok? We can't let them know about you, or worse, see who you are or where you are. Promise me you won't do that again."

Omori sniffed and nodded.

I turned to Dai. "Did you hear that?"

"I did," he said. "Which means she's useful to us again. That will be helpful in Qathab."

"You're going into Qathab?" Omori asked.

"And you're coming with us," Dai replied.

"No," I said. "No way. You heard what she said, the vessel could see right into her head. If we take her into Qathab they'll know instantly what she is, and they'll kill her. They won't want that threat. It's far too dangerous to let her go. She's no use to you dead, is she? I'll go with you."

"Omori would be more useful, and I can keep her at a safe distance."

"We don't even know what a safe distance is. I'll go with you. I can sense the vessels, not like Omori can, but when we walked into that interview room today I picked out instantly which one she was. And I knew her intentions. I could sense them. And that's without the danger of them reading me back. What kind of information do you think they could pull out of Omori when they can speak directly into her mind?"

"You could sense her intentions?" Dai asked.

"Yes. That's why I tried to get Kanak to put his gun down."

Dai gave a decisive nod. "Then you'll do. Omori might be more use if she's tracking down where the vessels go once they cross the border and what they're up to. I want you to focus on Honporo, that's where they seem to all be headed. I'll round up some volunteers to go with you."

He walked away without even waiting for an answer.

"Well, I guess that's decided then," I said. I turned to Omori. "When you get to Honporo, go to the colony. Ask about Tian, see if anyone's heard about him. It's a long-shot, I know, but he does have grandparents who are traders. It's worth a try, and I have to know. I have to know if he's still alive."

12

KIOTO

"I've never been out of Lobaya before," I said to Dai as we looked at the bit of land that stopped being Lobaya and became Merhan.

There was nothing to mark the border, and the road meandered casually across it as if it wasn't even aware of the transition. The wind blew Lobayan leaves into the fields of Merhan without a care, and the same sunshine blazed down equally on both countries. I didn't know what I had expected, but the absence of anything shocked me.

"Neither have I," Dai said.

"Really? A man of the world such as yourself?"

He laughed. "I'm not really that."

"My whole image of you is entirely shattered."

"Shut up and get in the car."

It took just a few hours to cross the narrow strip of northern Merhan before we were staring at the border with Qathab. This was a very different sight to the invisible border between Merhan and Lobaya.

A tall fence ran in both directions as far as I could see, a spiral of razor wire snaking along the top. It was spattered with signs warning of instant death should anyone attempt to breach the border. I couldn't help but wonder if this was Qathab keeping the Merhans out, or the Merhans protecting themselves from whatever lay beyond.

The road was blocked ahead by a rolling gate. A small building squatted by the roadside, surrounded with glass that gave the occupants uninterrupted vision in every direction. Just beyond, a large office building glared at us with windows ablaze with sunlight.

"You ready?" Dai asked.

I looked at him and I could see the cracks in his resolve. His brows furrowed down into eyes that wanted to turn and run. His hand tapped the dashboard next to the car's ignition button.

I nodded sharply. My own courage had left me long ago, and I had been relying on Dai's to get me through.

The car moved forward, and a border guard emerged from the building as the gate slowly rolled back. She waved us towards the larger office.

After having spent time at the Lobayan border, where I'd only spotted one female border guard, walking into Qathab was like walking into another world. I'd seen an old movie once about a land where there were only women, and this felt no different. I looked for a male face as we were led into the building, but there were none. I couldn't think what Qathab did with all its men.

The woman who led us inside stopped and turned to us.

"This way, please," she said to Dai, gesturing down a corridor. "And you," she said to me, "follow me."

I looked at Dai as we separated, but his eyes gave nothing of his feelings away this time. I balled up the fear in my stomach and tried to turn it into anger or at least a sense of being pissed off, but it stubbornly remained fearful. It would have to do. Perhaps I could draw something from it.

The interview rooms here were more like lounges; soft sofas, non-offensive artwork, potted plants. There wasn't even a mirrored wall. But I could feel eyes on me, beyond those in the room.

I was interviewed by the woman who had brought us inside, although it barely felt like that. As I was offered coffee and biscuits, it felt more like a friendly chat. I supposed that was how they got you to trust them and open up; by creating an illusion of benign informality. Perhaps that ball of fear would be an asset after all.

"Welcome to Qathab," she looked at my travel documents, "Kioto. I presume you've travelled here from Lobaya?"

I nodded.

"Have you been to Qathab before?"

I shook my head.

"Is it as hot in Lobaya as it is here? I am suffering in this heat, aren't you?" She laughed so lightly it was almost as if the sound had come from outside somewhere.

"I can't stand it."

She pointed to the ceiling. "At least we have air conditioning in here. I can turn it up if you'd like?"

"No, I'm fine, thank you."

"We don't have many traders coming here, but I know a lot about Lobayan traders. You're so traditional, keeping all the old ways. It's quaint, I love it. Have you got...." She gestured towards her right eye.

I pushed back my hair so that she could see my scars.

She shook her head. "Amazing that you still do that. It's considered quite barbaric here, now. But it's nice, in a way, that Lobaya keeps up with the traditions. So much tradition and custom was wiped out when Arukumbi was invaded."

I nodded. "It's still kept alive with the Arukumbi people."

"They don't really have much else to hold onto, I suppose. Much like you traders. Forced to scratch an existence at the far edges of the cities. The far edges of society. Treated like rats. It's not right."

"No."

"That's why I was surprised to see you with a rogue. I thought you guys were sworn adversaries."

"Normally, yeah."

"So how's that come about, you off on your

holidays with a rogue? Or is this more of a business trip?"

"I didn't really have a lot of choice."

She reached a sympathetic hand out towards me, stopping short of touching my leg. "He forced you to come?"

"Kind of. It's not like he has me at gunpoint, but if I try to leave, he will come after me. It's just a bit of an odd situation, really. It was my decision to come, but only because I didn't have a lot of options."

"It's tough to have your choices, your freedom, taken away from you."

"We've built this odd, tentative kind of friendship from it. It's hard to explain."

She nodded, and pushed the plate of biscuits closer to me. "It sometimes happens, people growing an attachment to a captor. Fondness, sometimes even love." She looked up at me.

"No." I shook my head. "No. He's old enough to be my father, my grandfather even. No."

"So, why's he brought you all the way here?"

"He's doing what rogues do. He's hunting down traders. Vessels in particular. He has quite a reputation for it."

"And he's interested in expanding his operation to Qathab?"

"It's more of a fact-finding mission at the moment."

The woman nodded slowly. "I see. Tell me a bit more about you. What colony are you from?"

I bowed my head. "Okaporo."

"Oh." Even in Qathab they knew.

"My whole family was killed that day. And then I continued my training in Kagosaka. But I was never happy there."

"Who was your brood mother in Okaporo?"

"Narata."

"And your rook?"

"Miya."

She nodded as if she knew the names. "Who were your parents?" she asked.

"Senetsu and Saji."

"And they were both killed in the massacre?"

I nodded. "Along with my little sister."

"That must have been so hard, finding yourself all alone in the world at just...you must have been young."

"Eight."

"Eight years old. How do you recover from something like that?"

"You don't. It just becomes part of who you are."

"And did they ever catch the rogues who did it?"

I huffed. "They didn't care. If anything, they saw it as a good thing; a few less traders to worry about."

She reached out towards me again. "So, you got no justice at all?"

"There's no justice for traders in Lobaya."

She leaned back and crossed her legs. "So I understand. But it doesn't have to be that way. That's not the situation here in Qathab. Traders are the government here. And we're keen to change things for our fellow traders in Lobaya. We're currently working there with a couple of more progressive colonies who are onboard with what we're trying to do. We want to see a better life for all traders. We want to see a fairer world for everyone, that's all. It's unjust that you're subjected to such a neglect of human rights just because you're born into a trader family. It's wrong, it's inhumane, it's immoral. An equal world is a better world for everyone."

I smiled grimly. "I can't disagree with that."

She smiled and nodded. "I thought you'd feel that way. You seem like you've got a good mind, and a strong will. You'd be a great figurehead at the front of our campaign for equal rights in Lobaya."

"I don't know. I try to stay out of it all. Politics, and stuff like that."

"Yet, here you are."

"It wasn't really my choice to be here."

"Then a few tricks and twists of fate brought you here. She has her funny little ways, and we might not always understand them. But you're looking straight at an opportunity here, Kioto, a chance to make life better for you and every other trader in Lobaya. A chance to front a campaign for equality and free your people from their social exclusion. Just imagine what a hero that would make you."

"I don't have much interest in being a hero."

"What do you want, Kioto?"

I sighed. "I want to go home."

"To Okaporo?"

I nodded.

"You and the other survivors have rights to that land. Rights that aren't currently recognised by your government, but we can change that. We can get you the deeds to the land that is yours. We can reclaim Okaporo together. You could have everything you've ever wanted. You could go home."

"It would really be that easy?"

She smiled. "I don't think I need to tell you what our vessels are capable of, do I?"

I shook my head. I thought about standing in that interview room, Kanak pointing his gun at Dai, how easy it would have been for the vessel to kill us both.

"What about Dai?" I mumbled, more to myself than to anyone else.

"We could deal with him, if you wanted us to. You just need to say the word. He poses no threat to us, and he's of very little consequence. It would be easy enough."

I frowned at my hands clasped in my lap. "No," I said. "Thank you, but no. How are your vessels so strong? I met a Lobayan vessel once, and she was nothing like yours are."

"We've been researching this for several generations, using genetic selection to purify and intensify their breeding. We've traced trader bloodlines back for centuries. Vessels in Lobaya, even traders, they're so impure now, the bloodlines are muddied and mixed. The heritage is diluted and weak. Flawed. Unworthy. But you, Kioto, you're different, and I think part of you has always known that you were special. Your family tree is one that we've been particularly interested in. You're a strong trader because of it, but we could help you become even more powerful. We've been experimenting with our abilities, learning to do things you wouldn't even believe possible."

I kept my eyes focussed on my hands. If I looked up at her I feared I might lose my will altogether.

"We had a supplier in Lobaya," she continued, "who agreed to supply us with the vessels, and the trader males that we were interested in. Ones that we could use in our research."

"A rogue?"

"No, a trader. One that understood the importance of what we were doing. But she failed to deliver, despite the financial investments she received for her colony. She let us down, and so we've had to take matters into our own hands. We're looking for more Lobayan traders to work with."

"I don't think I'm the person you're looking for."

"I think you're exactly the person we're looking for. Progressive, forward-thinking, and eager for change. Have I got that wrong about you, Kioto?"

"I'd love to see equality in Lobaya, but not like this. Not through murder."

"I'm disappointed that you think that way."

"There are lots of ways to fight for your rights. I don't think intimidation is the right one."

"And has dialogue worked for traders before? Did it work when rogues came and butchered everyone you loved and the government simply looked the other way? Did dialogue work for you then, Kioto? They will never listen unless you make them. And you don't make them listen with petitions, and protests, and pleasantries. They only understand one thing, and that's violence."

I shook my bowed head.

"What about the violence they've carried out against your people? Generations of persecution. That needs to be accounted for, and that's what we're doing. Merely giving them back everything they deserve. And those who stand against us will be met with the same violence, even if those people are our sisters."

"So that's it, you just kill anyone who gets in your way, no matter who they are?" I looked up at her then.

"No matter who they are." She spoke the sentence slowly, accenting each and every word.

I stood up. "And that's how you do things?"

She stood up. "That's how we do things."

"And what do you do with all the bodies?" I backed away. "They're going to start really piling up."

She smiled and shrugged.

13

MALIA

We had dozed through most of the journey, and when we arrived at the rogue camp just outside Honporo, we were all feeling groggy and disoriented.

Despite her protestations and obvious fatigue, Narata was swept away to some kind of meeting or debriefing, leaving us stood outside, unsure of where to go or what to do. Rogues certainly enjoyed coalescing. It was surprising they ever got anything done with so much talking.

Firefinch clambered up onto a wall and, from there, lifted himself onto the flat roof of a small outbuilding. It had a tiny, grubby window, and I peered inside. It may have been a toilet block once upon a time, but now, it seemed to be crammed with boxes and obsolete technology.

I followed Firefinch up, grabbing hold of his offered hand. He sat tight against me and lazily draped his arm around my shoulders. Omori joined us there.

"Look," said Firefinch, pointing. "There's Honporo. You can see the sparkle of the ocean on the far side."

Omori craned her neck. "I've never seen the ocean," she said.

I looked at her. "You were born in Okaporo. On the coast."

She blushed. "Right. I mean I don't remember seeing it before."

"I guess it's hard to have a connection to something you don't remember, however much you're told it's a part of you."

Omori nodded. "Yeah, Kioto goes on and on about Okaporo as if it's the only thing in the world. I just can't get excited about a bit of land. Even if my ancestors are there."

"Are you going to go with her if she manages to rebuild it?"

Omori shrugged. "Honestly, I don't really feel a great connection to anywhere. I guess Kumonayo was where I spent the most time, with my adoptive parents. But there was always a distance between me and them. I sometimes thought they might have been a little bit scared of me. I mean, there's no evidence that they've come looking for me at all. Maybe they were relieved when I disappeared."

I smiled as reassuringly as I could. "Maybe it's

time for you to make a home for yourself."

"Or maybe you don't need one," said Firefinch. "Maybe you're destined to be a wanderer."

I jabbed him with my elbow and he whimpered, rubbing his ribs.

"Either way," I said, looking back towards the glittering line of the sea, "Honporo looks beautiful from here. I've only ever seen it through a slit in the back of a wagon before."

"It's known as The Golden City," Firefinch said. "The buildings here are mostly built with the yellowish local stone, and when the sun catches it right, the whole city glows. That and it's where the lost riches of Lobaya are."

"You mean the lost riches of Arukumbi," I said.

"What riches?" asked Omori.

"People say there's gold on the seabed," I replied. "Honporo, or Mitmanimba as it was then, was the biggest port in the country, with merchant ships coming in and out every day. It's said to have also been the preferred port for pirates. There was certainly lots of rich pickings if you wanted to seize a vessel's cargo. The story goes that there was a huge ocean battle between pirates and merchants, and that every single one of the ships sank, and their treasures were lost to the sea. Some say the sand of Mitmanimba is actually gold, broken up by the sea over the years. Others say it was all carried away, and somewhere out in the world, there's a slick of treasure floating on the waves. Others say the beasts of the sea claimed it as their own." I shrugged. "It's a fascinating story."

Firefinch was staring at me, open-mouthed.

"What?" I asked.

"How do you know things like that?"

"Just because I didn't go to school, doesn't mean I wasn't schooled. The Arukumbi slaves look after one another, and we all receive a good education. It's amazing, I can even write my own name."

"Sorry... I didn't..."

I patted his leg. "It's ok. I'd probably assume the same thing. Our education is limited, though. We're taught everything there is to know about Arukumbi history, culture, politics, geography, but nothing about Lobaya. I had to learn that stuff myself, in secret. It wouldn't have gone down well with the elders."

"So what do you know about Honporo as it is now?" he asked.

"Enough to know why the Qathab vessels come here. It's the political centre of Lobaya, even though Aojima is its official capital."

"That's right." He nodded. "Officially, Aojima holds the ultimate power, with the ability to override even a strong majority vote, but in reality, they wouldn't dare stand against Honporo. They not only have strong government seats here, but they have double the seats of any other city. Originally, they were put in place as one government for the Lobayan citizens, and a second government for the Arukumbi citizens. This was the biggest Arukumbi city, and the hardest for the Lobayans to conquer. It was a condition laid down in law."

"But the Lobayans tricked the Arukumbi," I added.

"Right. It was also enshrined in law that no Arukumbi could be given a hereditary position, so they couldn't become a magistrate, those roles are simply handed down through families, and they couldn't become the minister, because they are elected from among the magistrates. So the Arukumbi presumed they'd be able to hold positions as either the alderman, or one of the readers. But, when the Arukumbi people found that they had been granted no rights to vote, there was no chance for any Arukumbi to enter government at all. No Lobayan would ever nominate them to become readers, or elect them as the alderman."

"That's so unfair," Omori said. "It must be hard to be in Honporo knowing how your people were tricked."

I shrugged. "It's the history of my people, but it doesn't really feel like my own history. I was born into slavery, both my parents were slaves, it's hard for me to imagine anything different. So I don't really feel angry about losing something I can't even imagine ever having. Does that make sense, or am I failing my people by not caring about this?"

Firefinch squeezed my shoulder. "You feel how you feel, you should never apologise for that."

"No, I get it," Omori said. "Kioto is always so angry about the injustice suffered by traders, but I just don't feel it. Who wants to live their entire life angry at the world?"

"Right," I said. "Go out and change it for the

better, or just put up with it."

We sat in silence for a moment.

"Do you think we're changing things for the better?" Omori asked.

I frowned. I didn't really know what we were doing, or who it might benefit. It didn't seem like any of this would change my situation.

"Sometimes," Firefinch said, "I think just changing things is enough."

"Maybe," Omori replied. "I just hope we're not making things worse. Or maybe things can't actually—" She stopped and frowned towards the floor.

"What is it?" I asked.

"There's a vessel here. In Honporo, I mean. I can feel her." She shook her head slightly. "I have to be careful, though. If I focus in on her too much then she'll know I'm here too."

"Don't you think she'll already know?" I asked.

"Probably, I guess. But I don't want to send her an invite to our door."

14

KIOTO

I sat in the car while Dai booked us rooms in one of the grubbiest-looking motels I'd ever seen. As a trader, I'd stayed in some very basic places, but this was beyond even that. The neon vacancies sign fizzed and crackled, lighting the small car park in a hot pink wash. I couldn't imagine they'd ever had the need to light the 'no' section of it. Most of the room doors had their numbers missing, and I couldn't help but think it might be deliberate; to confuse anyone should they ever witness a murder there.

Dai strolled back across the car park, a cyber card flashing in his hand. It lit up an annoyingly satisfied smile on his face. Either he really liked slumming it, or he really liked the idea of making me stay here.

I finally exited the car, and held my hand out to him.

"What?" he said.

"Where's my room key?"

"We're sharing."

"We're what?"

"Sharing. It means we'll be sleeping in the same room."

I screwed my face up. "Funny. Where's my key?"

"No, really. We've got a lot to talk about." He turned and strolled towards one of the rooms. "No sleeping on the job," he called back to me.

I tugged my bag out of the back seat of the car, and slammed the door. At least, I tried to slam it. They all had that soft close technology. Stupid thing stopped just before impact and quietly slid into place. I looked up and Dai was watching me, laughing. The car bleeped behind me, and I jumped. Dai laughed again.

I rammed my hands into my pockets, balling them round whatever rubbish they found in there. It was all I could do to stop myself from striding across the car park and slamming them into his face instead.

"Come on," he called. "You'll have plenty of time for teenage tantrums tomorrow."

As I drew level with him, I said "I'm not a teenager anymore. You stole my youth over the past three years, remember?"

"Maybe it's just your woman's time then."

I couldn't stop myself. My hand connected with his lip, and I saw blood splatter across his cheek. To say I was sorry would be a lie. He'd had that coming for a long time.

Without another word, Dai flashed the cyber card over the door lock and pushed his way into the room. He dropped his bag onto one of the beds (I was so relieved to see two of them) and disappeared into the bathroom at the back of the room. The light in there flickered as it turned on, illuminating a slice of the bedroom's grubby carpet.

I gently placed my bag on the other bed, but stayed standing. Looking around, I really didn't want to sit on anything in here.

The room was lit by two lamps that were mounted above the beds. Even in their half-hearted glows I could see sweat stains on the pillows.

Dai reappeared and leant against the door frame.

"You didn't have to hit me," he mumbled.

I turned away so that he couldn't see the look on my face. "You're right, I shouldn't have hit you."

"I can hear you smiling," he protested. He walked around me and sat on his bed. He kicked his shoes off, and drew his legs up under him.

"Why are we here?" I asked.

"What, here? In this motel?"

"Yes, for starters. We could have just slept in the car, in the air conditioning, let it take us back to Lobaya. Is everywhere in Merhan like this?"

"And miss out on this lovely experience?" He touched his lip with his fingers. It was beginning to swell.

I huffed. "It's like someone sucked all the air out of this room and poured in pure heat. Can't we at least open the window?"

"We're on the ground floor. In a place like this. You really want to open the window?"

"Seriously, why are we here? What funny little game are you playing this time?"

"For goodness sake, Kioto, it's a room, it's a bed. In a minute I'll go and buy us something unhealthy from the vending machine so that you can moan about that. Look how shit this place is, look how much you can grumble and whinge. You should be happy. Complaining seems to be your favourite pastime."

I flexed my hand, only then noticing the ache in it. "I have a new favourite now."

I looked down at the dark brown cover on the bed. I drew it back. The sheet underneath, which may have been white once upon a time, was almost the same colour. I covered it back up and finally sat down.

"So, what's the plan?" I asked.

"Well, in a minute, when my face has stopped throbbing, I'll go and see if I can find a vending machine."

I groaned and rolled my head. "Do you ever just give a straight answer?"

"If you ask a straight question. That one had a few too many possible answers."

"Maybe I need to hit you again," I muttered.

"Ok." He shifted on the bed to face me.

"Tomorrow morning we'll head back to Lobaya. We'll stop in and update Kanak on what we learnt in Qathab—"

"What I learnt," I corrected him.

He ignored it. "And then, well, I guess we'll head to Honporo to hook up with the others."

"And then?"

"What do you want from me? A five year plan?"

"You're using my sister, you're putting her through torture every day for your quest. And you're holding me captive. Don't you think I deserve to know where all of this is heading?"

"Sure, I'll let you know when I know."

"Do you even have an end goal?"

He grinned. "Is the destruction of all vessels and traders good enough for you?"

"I saved your life today. They asked me if I wanted them to kill you, and I said no. They'd have done it. I could have just given the word, and they'd have done it. You owe me your life."

"Every single day someone chooses whether or not to kill me, Kioto. I don't owe my life to anyone."

I sighed. "Fine. You know they told me they had a contact in Lobaya, a trader, who was meant to supply them with vessels and men?"

"Mmhmm."

"I'm certain it was Tokai. And I'm guessing that Omori was the vessel she promised them, but didn't deliver on."

"I would guess."

"So, by taking her memories, my parents

saved her life. Without even knowing the importance of what they'd done."

"Life's funny like that, isn't it?"

I sat in the semi-darkness and stared at the acidic pink glow that permeated the threadbare curtains.

"If only they knew."

"Kioto."

"Yes?

"Have you thought that it was even more than that? You said they were interested in your bloodline. Do you think they wanted your father too?"

"I hadn't even thought. And he saved himself from that by ending his own life."

"If, indeed, that's what he did."

"Why would Tokai kill him if he was promised to Qathab?"

Dai shrugged. "Maybe she didn't want to face them with only half of what she'd promised. Maybe it was easier to just keep making excuses. Or maybe everything just went horribly wrong. Speaking as a father—"

"Wait, you're a father?"

"Thought you had me all figured out, didn't you? But, speaking as a father, however devastated I was over my wife's death, accidental or not who knows, I, personally, wouldn't have just left my two girls out there alone. I'd have gone after them. Maybe he tried to leave, and Tokai tried to stop him."

A screen ignited between Dai's hands, lighting

his face in green. He glanced at it. "It's Narata. I'll take it outside."

As he closed the door behind him I stared at the imprint his weight had left in the bed. Shallow and empty.

15

MALIA

"I guess that's not a surprise," Narata said, once we'd told her what Omori had sensed. "We know the vessels have been making their way across Lobaya to Honporo, so it makes sense that there's at least one here already." She patted Omori's hand. "You did good."

"I withdrew my thoughts as soon as I felt her. Put up the barriers like you taught me."

Narata shook her head. "Not me. You already knew how to do that. Did Tokai teach you?"

"She used to come and see me at my adoptive parents' house, when I was younger, tried teaching me some things. But then she just stopped coming, I hadn't seen her in years. I guess she decided I was a lost cause with so many memories missing, and unable to be trained up."

"She continued paying your parents to keep you, though," Narata said.

"So she never completely gave up on you," I added.

"What do we do about the vessel?"

"Nothing." An older rogue stepped up behind Narata, and she sidestepped to make room for him. "Nothing. We wait until Dai tells us what we're doing. Just keep an eye...well, brain...whatever, on the situation, and inform us if anything changes."

"Perhaps we should head out to the colony and see if we can find anything out," Omori suggested.

"And we can enquire about Tian," I added.

Omori turned to me. "I forget that you knew him too. Kioto doesn't seem to like to talk about him at all."

"She misses him. They grew quite close while we travelled together. She probably blames herself too."

"I think I'll stay here," Narata said. "You two go. Having everyone thinking I'm dead has worked well so far, and it may be a good card to keep hold of."

Omori nodded.

Narata reached up to Omori's head and pulled her hair loose. She smoothed it down, and laid it over her face. "You should keep your eye covered. Pretend that you've got trader scars under there."

The colony at Honporo looked worryingly familiar. The houses were properly built, with pavements and roads running between them. You wouldn't be able to distinguish it from the city's suburbs. There was money here, which made me wonder where that money came from.

"It's just like Kumonayo," Omori whispered.

"Don't trust anyone here," I whispered back.

Faces appeared at windows and doorways as we ventured further into the colony. Children gathered in a hoard behind us, whispering and giggling.

And then a trader greeted us, pulling us into tight embraces before even knowing our names.

"Welcome, sisters," the trader said. "I am Shima, the brood mother here at Honporo. And you are most welcome."

Her eyes flicked between us. A pretend trader and her Arukumbi slave. I couldn't imagine what Shima might be thinking, but I read no hesitancy from her, no suspicion or mistrust. And it worried me. It worried me that she found nothing odd about us being together. Nothing odd about a trader bringing a carrier to her colony.

"Can we get you any refreshments at all? You're more than welcome to have a hot meal in our community building."

"No, thank you," said Omori.

She glanced at me, but I didn't meet her gaze. It was probably safer if Shima did believe me to be Omori's slave.

"Actually, we're after information," Omori continued.

"What can we help you with?"

"I hope you can help, it's a bit of an unusual

request. I'm looking for a young merchant named Tian."

Shima's face lit with recognition. "Tian? He's a trader, not a merchant, though. He lives here with his grandparents." She looked at me, and then back at Omori. "Of course, you must be Kioto. He's talked about you, and this must be Malia."

Omori nodded. "That's right. He's here?"

"Yes, his grandparents have been caring for him. I'm afraid you might find him quite changed, however. He's been through quite an ordeal. He arrived in the colony, out of the blue, bloodied and confused. I have no idea how he managed to get here at all. He's recovered a little, but he's very forgetful. He has a lot of memories missing. He might not make a lot of sense, but he certainly remembers the two of you. I'm sure it will do him a world of good to see you again."

Shima led us to a house at the far end of the colony. It sat near the edge of the cliffs, overlooking the sea below. Kioto would love it. A narrow gravel path led around the side of the building, and there, on a bench, looking out over the water, sat Tian.

I exhaled with a groan, my chest deflating so suddenly that I almost lost my balance. I wanted to run to him, throw my arms around him, sob into his chest with relief. I closed my eyes and bit back the tears. I was scared of how I might find him. Scared that he might have changed beyond recognition.

Tian turned, and stood up. He frowned for a moment, his face a crease of confusion. And then it lit with a smile. I remembered that smile, it was

Tian, completely Tian, and I couldn't hold the tears back anymore. They came hot and fast, and then his arms were around me, and we held each other so tightly. I was shaking, my body slumped heavily against his. I didn't want to ever let him go.

"Is Kioto here?" he whispered in my ear.

"Her sister is."

He pulled back and stared at me.

"But you need to pretend that she's Kioto."

He raised his face and looked past my shoulder, releasing his hold on me. He ran to Omori and scooped her into his arms, smothering her with kisses. When he finally put her down he whispered something to her, and she replied.

"I'll leave you to it," Shima said, looking satisfied. She bowed her head and left.

Tian turned back towards the sea glittering before us.

"I can see why my mother kept coming back here," he said. "Why she couldn't stay in Miyakata. And I see why Kioto loves the sea so much." He shook his head slightly. "It sounds silly, but I think I was meant to be here."

16

KIOTO

Before the car even stopped, we knew something was wrong. An ambulance was parked outside the Lobayan border office, its back doors closed. That was not a good sign.

Dai reached out and cancelled the parking automation, abandoning the car where it was. He leapt out and was inside the building before I'd even managed to unbuckle my seat belt.

The border office was in absolute chaos. People running, and yelling, and crying. No one even glanced at me as I made my way inside. The air was filled with terror, and it ate its way under my skin and made my heart race. I looked around for Dai, but all I could see was panic.

As I turned to go back outside, a hand grabbed

me around my neck, wrenching me backwards. My feet came clear of the floor as I slammed against the wall. An arm pressed down hard against my back, pinning me in place.

"What are you doing here?"

I opened my mouth uselessly, but there was no air left in my body to give me a voice. My cheeks burnt under tears, and my lungs heaved and gasped. I waited for the cold weight of a gun, I anticipated the bullet, but it didn't come.

"Let her go!"

I'd never been so relieved to hear Dai's voice. The body against me tensed and pressed harder, and then it was gone. Torn off me, and tossed away. I turned and fell into Dai's surprised arms.

"What—?" I gasped.

Dai lifted me away from him. "I shouldn't have left you, I'm sorry."

"Are you alright?" Kanak's hand was on my shoulder.

I nodded, shrugging him off. "I'm fine, I'm just shaken up."

"I'm sorry," said Kanak. "That should not have happened. Everyone's so jumpy, especially round traders. A guard just shot himself while interviewing a group from Qathab."

I shook my head. "He didn't shoot himself."

"No," replied Kanak. "I suppose not. But it's no excuse for your treatment. I'm sorry. It will be dealt with, I promise. Thankfully we've all had our guns impounded. I can't even imagine..."

"What will happen now?" Dai asked. "Surely

the government will do something now."

"I've shut down the border temporarily, but I've done that, we've had no instructions at all. A reader from Aojima has just arrived. The same one you spoke to before."

"A reader?" I asked. "A guard is dead, and they sent a data clerk?"

"They have a lot more authority than that," Kanak said, cocking his head. "But, you're right. You'd think they'd send the alderman, at least. I suppose it's a security thing."

"A security thing?" I gestured around us. "Look at this place. They need order, and instruction, and authority. We're way beyond rousing speeches and pats on the back. Where is he?"

"I don't think storming in is a good idea," said Dai.

I ignored him. "Where is he?" I asked Kanak again.

"Are you looking for me, trader?" The reader's voice boomed up the corridor, rising above any other sound.

I turned to him. "What are you going to do about this?"

"I don't answer to your kind."

"You need to answer to your employees, to your people. Right now, they're terrified, because you left them completely unprotected. It was only a matter of time before something like this happened."

"And your little mind games would have prevented this, would they?"

"You should have shut down the border ages ago."

"We do not give into terrorism."

I threw my hands into the air. "And how many more guards need to die?"

"We will not give into terrorism. The border remains open."

"Then you're putting the whole of Lobaya at risk, and for what? Keeping your import partners happy?"

"I don't answer to you, trader."

I stepped up to him. "Then, who do you answer to, Reader? Because your people want answers. They want to know what you're going to do about this. And I don't think 'nothing' is quite going to cut it."

The reader looked past me to Kanak. "We've called emergency meetings with the leaders in Qathab. We're doing what we can to resolve the situation."

"At least let Kioto teach us to protect ourselves," Kanak said. "Even if it only helps a little."

"I cannot, and will not trust a trader in the heads of government employees. Look what happened today."

"I cannot do that," I said. I screwed my hands into fists. I was hot with rage, shaking with it. "Let me protect them."

"No." He jabbed a finger towards me. "No. And if you defy me, you will be arrested and imprisoned. And you will never, ever be released. Do you understand?" He jabbed his finger towards Kanak. "Is that clear?"

The reader pushed past me without waiting for a reply, and went out to his waiting car.

Kanak placed his hand on my shoulder. "No matter what he says, I want you to help us. And the other guards do too. And we will do everything we can to protect you."

17

MALIA

As we sat down on the bench, Tian grabbed my hand and squeezed it. He didn't let it go again.

"What happened to you?" I asked. "After we separated?"

He shook his head. "It's all a bit fuzzy. But the rogues didn't catch me, not then. I was grabbed a few days later, but I don't remember who it was. They had a trader with them. They weren't very well trained though, either that, or they wanted to leave my head in tatters like this."

"They took memories from you?"

He nodded. "When they realised I didn't have the memory they wanted anymore, the one I gave to Kioto, they got angry and started pulling my mind apart." He gestured towards his temple. "And this is what they left me with. Oh, and this." He turned around, showing me the scar I'd only glimpsed earlier.

It was deep, the skin around it tight and creased. It ran from the base of his jaw, below his mouth, up across his cheek to his ear. They had also taken the bottom half of that.

"Oh, Tian." I squeezed his hand.

He shrugged. "I guess I'm closer to being a trader." He laughed tightly. "They kept me prisoner for a long time. I don't know how long, it honestly felt like years, but it may have only been a few days. Their trader, she just kept coming back and back for more." He pinched the bridge of his nose and closed his eyes for a moment. "I'm sure I can still feel her inside there sometimes."

"I'm so sorry," Malia said. "Maybe if we'd all stuck together—"

"Then we'd probably all be dead. Or like this. Half dead."

"You're not half dead."

"Besides, they'd have got the scratch, and Kioto would never have found Omori." He looked up at her. "I'm so glad she found you."

"Me too," Omori said. "And we have you to thank for that. Not that any thanks will ever be enough."

"No," I said. "They won't."

"Just seeing you alive and well is thanks enough," Tian said. "No more shivers?"

I smiled and shook my head. "Just my own thoughts in there now, and that's how it's going to stay from now on."

He nodded. "Good." He looked back out towards the sea, his thoughts apparently drifting again. "It's nice being off-grid. I can see why Kioto likes the nomad lifestyle."

"She doesn't like it," I said. "She has plans to return to Okaporo, to rebuild it."

Tian frowned. "Yeah, yeah, that's what I meant." He held up his hand. "No more implants." The tips of his forefinger and thumb were missing. I looked down, his other hand was the same.

"Did they do that? So that no one could trace you?"

He shrugged. "I don't remember. Sometimes I think I may have done it myself, so that they couldn't find me again."

"Oh, Tian." I turned away and gripped the front edge of the bench. The deep breath I took came back out with a tremble.

"Is Kioto coming? Is she safe?"

"She's doing very well, off on adventures. Saving the world, in fact. She's chasing vessels in Qathab. But I'm sure that when we tell her you're here, nothing will stop her from coming."

"She remembers me?" His face lit up at the thought.

"Of course. She hasn't stop pining over you for three years."

"Has it only been three years? It feels more like three lifetimes."

"Just three years," I confirmed. "Are you happy here?"

"Yes. Yes, I am. They tell me I was a mess when I arrived. My face in tatters, my mind even worse. Shima's tried her best to piece it back together, but there wasn't a lot there to work with. I don't really remember much of it, and I have no idea how I got here. They say I just wandered into the colony one day, out of the blue, unannounced." He shrugged. "Maybe it was just good luck."

"Maybe it was fate."

"Perhaps. What did you say Kioto was doing?"

"Chasing vessels in Qathab. But you can't tell anyone that. We don't know who we can trust anymore."

"I've heard that word." He frowned, his eyes flicking from side to side as he searched through his memories. "Here. Here in Okaporo."

"Honporo."

"Yeah, that's what I meant. Honporo. Honporo. Shima's said it, and my grandparents."

"Can you remember what they said?"

"There were visitors, lots of strangers coming." He balled his hand into a fist and bounced it against his thigh. "It's going, the thought's going."

"That's ok."

"No, it's not. The strangers, they look different. They look... The way they look at you... It's not right."

My eyes met Omori's. I could see the concern in her face. The same as I felt in my gut.

"My grandparents say not to worry, that they're here to help us, to help all traders. It doesn't feel like that. I'm scared of them. I can't help it. It doesn't... It doesn't feel right..." He lifted his eyes to the ocean again. "It's so pretty here. Don't you think it's pretty?"

"It is. Very pretty. Kioto will love it."

He nodded. "Is she here?"

I squeezed his hand. "She will be. Soon."

18

KIOTO

Kanak placed a heavy hand on my shoulder. "Thank you," he said. "I know you're risking a lot by teaching us that."

"I'm not sure that it'll do any good."

"It's taken this place from panic to calm, that's enough good for me. Just having something to do, when the government have given us nothing, that goes a long way in itself. And you can trust everyone here. No one will tell anyone what you've taught us today."

"Kanak!" someone further down the corridor shouted.

"Excuse me. Safe journey." He gave Dai a hug and patted me on the shoulder once more before disappearing through a doorway.

I looked up at Dai. "Where are we headed next? Still thinking of going straight to Honporo?"

Dai nodded. "I guess that's our best bet. Meet up with the others and decide from there."

I stepped towards the front door and it slid open, filling the corridor with the humidity of summer. I was reluctant to leave the nice, cool border office behind, but it was only a few steps to the air conditioned car. Not all technology was bad.

Kanak's hand was on my shoulder again, but it wasn't patting this time, this time it was grabbing, and pulling me backwards. I stumbled, barely managing to stay on my feet. Without a word, he spun me around, and pushed me back down the corridor.

"You can't leave," he said. "There's already a guard outside waiting to arrest you."

"You said no one here would betray her," Dai said.

"They didn't. This isn't about you teaching us mind blocking techniques. This is because of the reader you screamed at earlier."

"What exactly is he having me arrested for?"

"Attempted murder," Kanak replied with a grimace.

"What?"

"That's crazy," Dai said, grabbing hold of my wrist.

"He stepped off the pavement straight in front of a bus. The auto brakes did their job, he's completely unharmed, but it was a close call. He's claiming that you put the thought in his head to do it. That you tried to kill him."

"That's insane," I said.

"I know," replied Kanak. "But it was a really busy street, lots of people saw what happened. I guess he's just embarrassed."

"He's claiming I tried to kill him because he's embarrassed? I can't even do stuff like that."

"I know you can't. I've had a vessel in my head, I know what it feels like. And when you were testing my mind blocking it was nothing like the same. But they see no difference between traders and vessels. Look, we've got some old holding cells underground. They've not been used in years, most people don't even know they're there. They're full of junk now, and probably rats, but you can hide down there. I'll tell them that you've already gone."

"No," I said. "I need to face them. They'll think I ran, it will only make me look guilty."

"You're a trader," said Dai. "They're not going to give you a fair trial, or, probably, any trial at all. You can't protest your innocence, they won't believe you. You need to hide, Kioto. In their minds you're already proven guilty."

19

KIOTO

I could see the glint of Dai's eyes in the darkness, but couldn't read his expression. He was holding both of my hands, and I wondered if he was as terrified as me. Whether he really cared, or if he was just protecting an asset. I wanted him to care, I realised, and the thought surprised me.

Above us, footsteps marched back and forth. I imagined them searching for me, turning the place upside down.

"What do we do if they come down here?" I whispered. I wasn't even certain I wanted an answer. The question hung in the darkness for a moment, unanswered. Perhaps unanswerable.

"You have two choices," Dai finally replied. "You give yourself up, or you fight. Only you can decide which."

I clambered to my feet and, with the light from my phone, began to search the row of cells. There were boxes and boxes of paperwork, stacks of chairs, odd lampshades, mugs, old coffee machines, outdated computer equipment, old uniforms.

"What are you looking for?" Dai asked.

"I don't know, but I'll know when I find it. I mean, this is the border office, there's got to be something of use around here."

I clambered over a desk that had been abandoned in a doorway, and that was when I found it.

"Aha," I said.

Dai peered over the desk to where I was crouched. "What have you found?"

"A big bag of old riot gear."

He laughed. "Are you serious?"

I held up a bullet proof vest, the words 'BORDER GUARD' printed across it. I tossed it to Dai, and pulled out another for myself. I slipped it over my head and strapped it around my waist.

Dai held up his vest and looked at it. "You know, I always wondered what you're supposed to do if they simply shoot you in the head. Never happens in the movies, they always aim for the chest. Even when they know they're wearing one of these. It always struck me as odd."

"Shut up, Dai," I said, and tossed him a baton. He weighed it in his hand. "Is this really the best you can find?"

"What are you expecting?" I asked him. "Maybe a hidden switch that reveals an arsenal of weaponry behind a wall? A tank perhaps?"

"Then I guess we'll just have to make the best of it."

I climbed back over the desk and we positioned ourselves on either side of the stairs that led down from the entrance hatch. I lifted the baton and held it poised. And then we waited.

20

MALIA

I glanced back over my shoulder as we walked out of the Honporo colony. It ached to leave him, but at least I knew where he was, and I knew he was safe for now.

"It's so sad," I said. "I can't believe they put him through so much. They had no reason to keep hold of him when they realised he didn't have the scratch anymore. They tortured him for their own satisfaction. At least Kioto will be happy to hear that he's safe."

"She will," said Omori. "But that's all we'll tell her. She doesn't need the worry while she's so far away. We won't tell her what they did to him. She'll only blame herself."

"Agreed. She doesn't need to know until she

gets here."

"Kioto!" We turned as someone shouted. Shima ran towards us. "Kioto!" she called again, waving her arms.

We walked back towards her.

"I want to show you something," she said. "I have something that might help you to understand a little more about what happened to Tian. It could help him." She cocked her head and we followed her.

She unlocked the door to her house, and led us inside.

"We've been trying to find ways to help Tian. You saw how confused and distressed he is."

"He didn't seem distressed," I said.

"Then you must have caught him on a good day. I've been searching for his memories for some time, and I finally found a carrier who had some of them. I tried to give them back to him, but he's so untrusting, he wouldn't let me. He wouldn't even let his grandparents do it."

"That's understandable," said Omori. "He told us about the trader, what she did to him. He must be terrified."

Shima nodded. "He is. But I wonder if he'd trust you. If you could give them back to him. It's not all of his missing memories, not by far, but he's under my care now, and even if I spend years piecing him back together bit by bit, then I'm willing to do that. His grandparents are respected members of this colony, and we'll do what it takes to help Tian."

"I'll certainly give it a go. It's worth a try." Omori looked at me, her eyes full of hope. I knew what she was thinking; that maybe Kioto would find him in a far better state than we had.

"Through here." Shima led us to a bedroom. A carrier was lying on the bed, her eyes closed. It was an odd feeling to see all this from the other side.

"She's a brand new carrier, and not very well trained, well, I'm not sure she's had any training at all. She was so scared I had to sedate her. That means you'll have to go in deep and find Tian's memories for yourself, they won't be pushed forward for you. You won't meet any resistance though, it should be easy enough."

Omori glanced back at me. "It happens," I said. "Some merchants don't care enough to train their carriers. They just force memories in, and rip them back out." I shuddered. "It's barbaric."

"Ok," Omori said. "Oh, but I don't have anything with me for a dedication."

"You can use mine," Shima said. "It won't be quite the same, of course, but we need to work with what we've got. For Tian's sake."

Shima's dedication items were already laid out on a side table: the bowl, heather, rabbit pelt, and pebble. I could smell that the bowl contained salt water. Traders were so deeply connected to the places they lived. I wondered if I'd ever feel that connected to somewhere.

"Perhaps you should leave us?" Shima said to me.

"No," Omori said quickly. "I'd like her to stay. She's seen this so many times, she won't distract me."

Shima nodded.

Omori placed her fingers on the rim of the bowl, and closed her eyes. "My life was given by you, and will be offered up to you again. I will treasure your gift and use it in a way that glorifies your names."

She moved her hand to the heather. "My roots were chosen by you, and your wisdom has set me on the correct path. I faithfully walk that path for you, and do so in your names."

She touched the pelt. "My family was given by you, and will be offered up to you again. They are my strength, my home, and my responsibility. I will love them in a way that honours your names."

She touched the pebble. "You gave me free will, you gave me choices, and I will seek to mould my life with grace and truth. I will be influenced only by these things, and influence others by them. I choose to respect your teachings and follow your ways. For all of this I give thanks and ask for your blessing. Please stand with me as I perform this rite. Let my hands be your hands, my breath, your breath, and my heart, a vessel for your presence. In your names, I ask this."

I'd only seen the Dedication performed a small number of times, but Omori's recital was flawless. I was relieved for Narata's insistence on doing things correctly, according to the traditions, so that Omori didn't betray her true identity.

Omori crossed to the bed and placed one hand on the carrier's forehead, and the other on her stomach.

"Remember to go all the way in," Shima said. "Find every one of Tian's memories that you can."

Omori nodded and closed her eyes. She frowned as she pushed her way into the carrier's head. And then her mouth opened, and her body jolted.

I'd seen many extractions, and this wasn't right. I stepped forward, reaching out to her.

Shima grabbed my shoulders and pulled me out of the room, closing the door behind us.

"You're not a trader," she said to me. "You have no business being here. You should leave."

"What's happening? She needs help."

"She doesn't need help from... whatever you are. A carrier with nothing to carry? Who emptied you out, smudger? Yes, I know who you are. I've been through Tian's memories, and no one just recovers from the shivers. Who emptied you out?"

"That's none of your business," I said sharply.

"And this is none of yours. Leave my colony."

"Kioto needs me."

"Leave, or I'll call the authorities. I'm sure they'll be interested in a slave wandering around like a free citizen. And they'll be interested in why Kioto has you."

"I won't leave Kioto."

"Yes. You will. Or I'll kill you both."

21

MALIA

I felt like I'd been pacing the entrance to the colony forever, watching the road for any sign of Omori. My eyes were beginning to ache, and the darkening skies threw shadows that I mistook for a person several times.

But the colony remained eerily still. A few lights showed behind curtains, but there was no sound, no people, nothing but the constant breathing of the sea beyond.

I flexed my fingers and wished that I had implants, or at least a phone, anything, so that I could call Narata. She'd know what to do. But for now, all I had was waiting, and I'd wait all night if I had to.

Stars were beginning to glint in the deep purple

sky above me. I looked around for the moon, but it was absent. Looking the other way. I wondered if the High were looking the other way too.

I glanced back at the road, and a shadow moved across it, stumbling, or running. But this wasn't another shadow trying to trick me, this was Omori.

I ran to her, and she clung to my arm, her legs barely holding her weight.

"What happened?" I asked, panic rising through me.

"I'm fine," she whispered. "Really, but I need you to help me walk, I need to pretend I'm hurt."

"What did she do to you?"

"That wasn't a carrier with Tian's memories. And she wasn't sedated because she was scared. She was sedated so that I didn't realise she had the shivers. She was a smudger, Malia, completely topped out. It was a rush, Shima tricked me. That's why we need to pretend I'm dying."

"She tried to kill you?"

"Well, she tried to kill Kioto."

22

KIOTO

I leaned my head back against the wall behind me and sighed. I rubbed my eyes to try and bring the world back into focus. I must have dozed off again.

"It feels like we've been here forever," I whispered.

"Hiding out isn't so much fun once the adrenaline wears off, is it? Once your arms get tired from holding a damn baton above your head."

"What time is it?"

Dai opened a small screen. "Half nine."

"It feels like we've been stuck down here for days. Do you think Kanak's forgotten about us?"

"Maybe he's been arrested."

"Or killed. Maybe everyone up there is dead."

"Don't you think we'd have heard a gun fight?"

"Maybe it was a nice neat firing squad. They took them outside, lined them up, and 'pop, pop, pop', quick and tidy."

"In that case, I hope you like the taste of toasted rat."

"Do you think we should just sneak a look upstairs? Just a little peek? See what's happening?"

"Kanak will come for us when he can. Besides, he locked the hatch from the outside. We're completely trapped, and only he knows we're here. Probably."

"Stop it." I shoved him. "I hope he brings some food when he does come."

"Maybe we'll have to resort to cannibalism."

"I really don't want to be stuck down here forever. Can you call him?"

"No signal. Even if I did have one, it would be a risk. We wouldn't know who might be listening in."

We both jumped as the hatch above us rattled. I stood up and raised my baton again, but between my sweating hands, and the tremors running up and down my arms, I could barely grip it at all. My heart pulsed so loudly in my ears that I couldn't even think.

"Dai?" called out Kanak.

"Mercy!" I cried out, my baton clattering to the floor. I dropped to my knees, my chest heaving as my lungs desperately sought oxygen.

Light cut through the darkness as the hatch was opened, and I snapped my eyes shut, blinded for a moment.

"Are you guys alright?" Kanak asked.

I looked up at him. "You took your time."

Dai clambered up the stairs and took a deep breath of the fresh air above. "Her sarcasm's still working, so that's a good sign."

I grabbed Kanak's offered hand, and clambered out into the room above.

"I'm so sorry," said Kanak. "They've only just left. They sat outside for ages before doing anything, and then they requested that every weapon on the premises was surrendered. They acted like there was a ticking bomb here, and they wouldn't come in until they knew it was disarmed. Then there were interviews and interviews and interviews and reports and paperwork. You know what the government is like. If it's not duplicated and triplicated they're not happy. I'm sorry. You must be starving."

"I could eat anything right now," I said.

Kanak led us to the staff canteen where a whole wall of vending machines hummed and tempted. We had a feast of packeted sandwiches, and fruit that had been oddly shrink-wrapped despite having its own protective skin. We ate crisps and chocolate, and guzzled fizzy drinks. And all of that sugar-filled food, the colours, the preservatives, the flavourings, tasted like the best food I'd ever eaten.

"I honestly don't know if I feel better or worse now," I said, leaning back and resting my hands on my over-filled stomach.

"I know what you mean," said Dai.

"How did the authorities leave things?" I asked Kanak. "Are they still looking for me?"

"There's a warrant out for your arrest. If they catch you, they will imprison you, probably without trial, or hope of release. They'll want to make an example out of you with them being so helpless against the actual vessels. They can finally look like they're doing something. But I can't see them actively pursuing you. I'd say keep your head down, stay out of the city centres, don't draw attention to yourself, and you'll probably stay under their radar."

"For how long? The rest of my life?"

Dai tapped the table with his finger. "Until this is all over. We will finish this, Kioto, and clear your name."

"Well, forgive me if I start looking for caves to live in, ok?"

"I hear there's some lovely residential caves around Kagosaka."

"There, I'm all set for my life as a fugitive."

"We will sort this," Kanak said.

I could tell he wanted to mean that, and I wanted him to as well. But we both knew this was far above his pay grade. Even Dai didn't have friends in high enough places to help me.

"Perhaps I should've taken up their offer in Qathab," I said grimly.

A small screen appeared by Dai's hand. He looked at it. "It's Narata. Let's find out what's going on in Honporo. Perhaps she'll even have some good news."

He pulled his hands apart and the screen

enlarged, showing Narata's face.

"Hi, Narata," Dai said. "How are things by the seaside?"

"Not as pleasant as you might expect. I'm guessing you're back in Lobaya now?"

"Yep, we're at the border office."

"Is Kioto there?"

I scooted my chair over so that I was on camera too.

"I'm here."

"Omori and Malia went to the colony today, and guess who they found?"

"Tian? He's at the colony?"

"Right. That's where his grandparents are from. He's living with them, and enjoying being by the sea apparently."

"How is he?"

"Doing really well, according to Omori and Malia. He was asking after you."

"We'll be there soon, I think." I glanced at Dai.

"That's right," he confirmed. "We'll leave here in a few minutes and head towards you."

"Something else happened at the colony that you need to know about," Narata said. "The brood mother, Shima, took Omori into a room where a carrier was sedated on the bed. She forced a rush onto her."

"She tried to kill her?" I said.

"Actually, she tried to kill you. Omori was pretending to be you."

"What happened?"

"Omori acted the part and stumbled out of the

colony. They think you're dead, Kioto."

I nodded. "Clever girl. Why would they want me dead?"

"I'm guessing it's to do with the scratch you and Tian never delivered. The one revealing Omori's whereabouts. The colony here is just like Kumonayo; wealthy. I'm guessing Shima is in this along with Tokai."

"You're both ghosts now," said Dai.

"Let's keep it that way," I said. "People have kept saying about traders using topped out carriers as weapons, killing other traders with a rush, but I hadn't believed it. I just couldn't imagine a trader doing that to one of their own." I shook my head. "How fitting that everyone thinks I died from a rush. Just like my mother did." My chest felt empty, as if my insides had all disappeared once. What was left behind was cold, cavernous, like staring into darkness. "Do you think Tokai did it? Do you think Tokai killed my mum with a rush?" I looked at Dai. "Do you think she could have killed both of my parents?"

Dai shook his head. "I don't know. I guess we'll never know. Unless you can get her to admit to it."

I looked back at Narata's face on the screen. "We might take a little longer getting to Honporo," I said. "I want to make a detour first." I looked at Dai. "We're going to Kumonayo."

"What about saving the world?" he asked.

"That can wait."

He grinned. "The world doesn't wait for anyone."

23

KIOTO

I stared out of the car at the lights of the Kumonayo colony. I hadn't imagined I'd ever come back here, but I needed to finish this.

"What's the plan?" Dai asked.

"I don't know."

"Are you really going to walk in there with no idea what you're doing?"

"I want to see how I feel when I'm face to face with Tokai."

"Kioto, you can't just act on hatred."

I turned to him. "Why not? Your people have made a career out of it."

I pressed the door release button and climbed out into the cool evening air. Before I had even realised what I was doing, I leaned back in, flicked open the glove box, and pulled out Dai's gun. It was heavier than I'd expected, and as I dropped it into my coat pocket, I stumbled with its sudden weight.

As I walked away I heard Dai shout after me. "Do you even know how to use that?"

I didn't, and hoped that I wouldn't need to. But there was already a warrant out for my arrest, for an attempted murder I would be convicted of, so what did I have to lose?

I walked into Tokai's house without knocking, and I enjoyed seeing her jaw dangling open at the sight of me. She raised a shaking finger.

"No... but you're dead. Shima... you're supposed to be dead."

I smiled. "That's the funny thing about sisters, they often look alike."

"That was Omori? Shima killed Omori?"

"She's a vessel. All Shima did was save that poor carrier's life."

"She... she's been trained up? But how?"

"I found her memories. You know that smudger I had with me? They were in her. You never even thought, did you? You judged me by your own standards, figured that I was walking around with a loaded weapon, but actually, Malia was the key to everything. And you let her slip right through your fingers. It was all rather serendipitous really. I guess the High wanted me to find Omori's memories. They're obviously not very happy with you. And neither are your associates in Qathab. It seems like you didn't deliver on a few promises."

"How do you know about that?"

"I know everything, Tokai."

Her eyes flicked from side to side as she searched her head for answers. I saw the spark on her face when she saw one. She straightened up.

"And I know quite a lot about you, too. I know you've been hiding with rogues." She said the word as if it tasted sour on her tongue. "That's a dangerous game. Don't you know that they'll betray you, sooner or later, because that's what rogues do. They'll string you up by the neck along with Omori. But, well, at least you'll die side by side with your sister at last. But it's a strange choice in allies, Kioto, after rogues have taken everything from you. They even carved up your little friend Tian after you left him to their mercy to save your own skin."

"What?" My mouth was dry, my tongue like driftwood.

"So your friends didn't tell you about that, then? He's not quite the person you remember him as. Not any more. Rogues took everything from you. Your home. Your family. They killed everyone you loved."

"Not everyone."

Tokai waved a hand dismissively. "Fine, you have your sister back, but that hardly makes a family. And you'll never have your home back, and that's what really eats you up inside, isn't it? Are you homesick, Kioto?"

"I will return to Okaporo."

Tokai smiled. "Haven't you heard? The authorities reclaimed the land. They built on it. They dug up your ancestors and tossed their bones out with the rubble. Your precious home is probably underneath the car park of a casino now."

"You're lying."

Tokai shrugged. "Go and see for yourself."

I tugged the gun from my pocket and pointed it at her. "Kneel down," I said.

Slowly, Tokai knelt. She bowed her head and raised her hands.

I pressed the muzzle of the gun against her skull. It filled me with a sense of power that sat uncomfortably inside me.

"Did you kill my parents?" I asked.

She didn't answer.

I pushed the gun forward, forcing her head to one side. "Did you kill my parents?"

"The traders from Qathab were making too many demands, impossible demands, and your parents were ruining everything. They'd done an extraction on Omori, a child, ripped the memories out of her."

I felt something familiar then. A sense of déjà vu. I'd had this feeling before. Not the feeling of holding the gun, not the feeling of my own intent, but the feeling of someone else's. I wasn't the only one focussing on it. And now I knew what I had to do.

"You don't even have the courage to admit what you did, do you?" I said. "A coward to the end."

"Kioto, I know you're angry, and confused, but it's for the good of all traders."

"The greater good?" I leaned in closer to her.

"It just seems that I've paid a higher price than most."

"Don't kill me, Kioto. You're better than this. Better than those rogues. Although they seem to have rubbed off on you."

I withdrew the gun. "I'm not going to kill you, because I want to be able to see the look on your face when all of your plans come undone. That's what Omori's doing right now, in Honporo, unravelling everything."

Tokai slowly rose to standing. "I won't let all of my plans fall apart so easily, Kioto. You should want to see traders in charge at last, it's owed to us, it's what we deserve."

"I do want to see traders treated fairly, and equally, but not like this. Not through fear and death."

"Stop being so naive, you're a grown woman now. That's how power is won. That's how the Lobayans took it from the Arukumbi, and that's the only way to get it for ourselves. We have them running scared, all it will take is one final strike."

"Is this what you want? All this in-fighting? Traders killing traders?"

"I'm willing to do whatever it takes. Even if I have to kill Omori. It would be easy enough, just one touch from a Qathab vessel."

"That would be suicide. The touch would kill the Qathab vessel too."

Tokai shook her head. "Omori isn't nearly strong enough to do that. No Lobayan vessel ever could be."

24

KIOTO

I climbed back into the car, and the door quietly slid into place behind me.

"What happened?" Dai asked.

I pulled the gun from my pocket. Its grip got caught on the lining, and I wrenched it free, almost dropping it. I opened the glove box and placed it inside.

"What happened?" Dai asked again.

I turned to him, his face disappearing into shadow as the interior light dimmed and went out. I was grateful for the darkness. There were some things that could only be said in the security of darkness.

"You need to take me to the Kagosaka colony."

Dai tapped it into the route setter, and an

electronic voice confirmed the selection. The car hummed and began to move.

"Did you kill Tokai?" Dai asked.

I shook my head. "No. But I think I have a way to end all of this."

25

MALIA

Omori reached over the small table between us and grabbed a fistful of chips from my plate. I swiped my fork at her, missing by miles.

"Oh, is this a free-for-all?" Firefinch laughed, grabbing his own handful of food.

I stabbed him in the arm with my fork.

"Hey!" he cried. "Why doesn't she get that kind of vicious behaviour?" He gestured at Omori.

I grinned. "Sisterhood."

"Then what chance do I have?"

"Sorry." I patted Firefinch's arm. "There's absolutely nothing you can do about it. It's a sacred bond. Can't be broken."

Omori shook her head slowly. "Sorry."

We looked up as Narata walked in.

"Fun's over," whispered Omori. "Time for work."

Narata sat herself down at the table. "Omori," she said. "I've just spoken to Kioto. She's not coming straight to Honporo, not just yet. She says she'll be here in a day or two. But she needs you to pinpoint the vessel's location here, if you can."

"But that means I'll have to connect with her," Omori said. "And if I do that, she'll probably be able to pinpoint my location too."

Narata nodded. "I know. But you need to do this. With a bit of luck we can catch her by surprise, shut the link down before she even realises what's happening. And then we'll move you."

"Ok. I'll see what I can do."

Firefinch leaned across the table and opened up a screen with his fingers. He brought a map of Honporo on it.

Omori took a deep breath. "Here we go." She closed her eyes.

We all watched her intently. I waited for something, some kind of sign of the connection. A jolt, a whimper, a scream. I didn't even know what I was expecting.

Omori's eyes flickered open. She pointed to the map. "There. She's there."

Firefinch zoomed the map in, and Omori pointed to a single building.

"You're sure?" Narata asked.

"Positive," Omori replied. "She asked me who I was."

"What did you say?" asked Narata.

"Nothing."

Narata stood and patted Omori's hand. "Good girl." She looked at Firefinch. "Take Omori somewhere, anywhere. Just don't tell anyone where you're going with her. Even I don't need to know. Just get her somewhere safe. I'll call you if I need any more information on the vessel's location." She looked at me and cocked her head towards the door. "Malia, you come with me."

26

MALIA

The building Omori had pointed to turned out to be an abandoned warehouse near the docks. Its brick facade was split by a sign that stretched the full width of the building, illegible after years of sunshine and salt air. Its large windows were speckled with broken panes.

"Are you sure this is right?" I asked Narata.

"This is the building she said. Let's trust her. Malia, I need you to play the part of the smudger one last time. Stay behind me, head bowed, and don't say anything."

I nodded.

"Come on then." For a moment, Narata didn't move, as if she were building up courage first. With a nod of her head, she strode forward and slipped through the large front doors that stood ajar.

The interior was dark and empty. Despite the broken glass in the windows, the sun still struggled to intrude on the space. Or perhaps it simply had no desire to be there. I could sympathise with that.

Narata walked further into the gloom, and I was grateful to be able to walk behind her.

"What do you want?" The voice seemed to come from everywhere and nowhere. Narata's head reeled around as she tried to locate the speaker.

"I want to speak with the vessel," Narata replied. Her voice was steady and strong, and I couldn't help but feel impressed. I doubted mine would have been more than a squeak.

"You know what I am?" the voice asked.

"Yes."

"Then you know what I can do?"

"Yes. Tokai sent me to you."

"Tokai. What does she want now?"

"A chance at redemption. She's on her way to Honporo. She has the vessel that she promised you. Omori of the Okaporo colony."

"Tokai told us that she was dead."

"The girl was useless, she'd had several memories ripped, but those memories have now been restored to her. She's been trained."

"We no longer have any interest in her. Our focus has changed, and it's too little too late. Tokai will not be forgiven her betrayal."

Narata shifted her weight. "Tokai was prepared for rejection, and in that case, she'll be using Omori as a weapon."

I knew that I'd never forget the laugh that came out of the darkness then. It was so cold, so callous, as if some ancient, primitive evil had opened its jaws to crow.

"No Lobayan vessel has the strength to be any threat to us."

"This one is from a strong bloodline, a bloodline that you, yourselves, wanted to use. So you had better be certain of yourself. Omori has already managed to pinpoint your location for us, so I wonder what else she can do? Think about that."

No reply came.

Narata turned towards me and gestured that it was time to leave. "We'll let you know when Tokai's ready to meet," she said as we left.

27

KIOTO

Narata was already stood outside when we arrived at the Honporo rogue camp. She greeted Dai with a long hug.

"Did you keep her safe?" she asked him.

He gestured towards me. "She's still in one piece, isn't she?"

Narata pulled me into an embrace. "Did he look after you properly?"

"Yes, yes, I'm fine." I pulled free of her grip.

"Besides," said Dai, "she was technically killed here in Honporo. On your watch." He patted Narata on the shoulder.

I laughed. "That's true, actually."

Narata looked from Dai to me and back again. "Looks like you've rubbed off on each other a bit too much. I'll have to keep you separated from now on. Too much trouble. Anyway, did you manage to find some transport for everyone?"

"Dai sorted it out."

Dai gave a quick bow. We turned and stepped out of the way as an auto bus pulled up. It stopped, and the doors slid open. The Kagosaka traders filed off and huddled together, looking around them.

Narata pulled me aside. "This is all? There's only about twenty. Is it going to be enough?"

"It was all I could convince to come. And we better just hope it's enough. Where's Omori?"

"Firefinch has her hidden somewhere in the city. I don't know where."

"Did you tell her the plan?"

"No."

"I'll give Firefinch a call. I'll go and speak to her myself. If she doesn't agree to this, then the whole plan is off. She'll be risking everything, so it's her decision."

"What happens if she says no?"

I shrugged. "Then we'll have to think of something else."

28

KIOTO

I hugged Omori tightly. "You don't need to agree to anything."

"What choice do we have?"

I moved her away from me, holding her at arm's length. "Not 'we'. This is your choice, and only your choice. We have no idea what's going to happen. No idea if the traders will offer any kind of protection at all."

Omori frowned and shook her head, just the slightest movement. "If it's a choice between the Qathab vessels winning, and... well... my head possibly exploding, I honestly think I'd rather take the exploding head. I've seen inside their minds, and there's a darkness there that I don't like. They talk about this being for the good of all traders, that they're fighting for equality, but that's not the sense I get from them. There's a deeper, darker purpose that they're keeping very well hidden. Yeah, I'll take the exploding head."

I pulled her into another tight embrace, unsure which of us was shaking more. "You're the bravest person I know."

"I get it from my sister."

"Hardly, the risk is all yours."

Omori pulled away and shrugged. "If I die, then it will be nothing to me anymore. But you'd be all alone again. You'll have lost everything for the second time. You're the one that's risking everything." She spoke bravely, but she couldn't stop the tears rolling down her cheeks.

"You're an idiot," I said, unable to hold back the tears of my own. I took hold of her hands, the need to touch her overwhelming me. "But I love you. And I'll be by your side the entire time. I'm not going anywhere."

Omori frowned and looked up at me. "Another vessel's just arrived in the city."

29

ℳALIA

Narata could move impressively quickly for her age. She also had a surprisingly strong grip as she grabbed hold of my arms.

"Omori's picked up the second vessel. They're here, and they're on their way to the colony. Omori's contacting the first vessel to tell her Tokai's ready to meet. Kioto wants us to watch, to make sure everything goes to plan. Are you ready?"

I nodded, not trusting my voice to actually say the word 'yes'.

30

KIOTO

I knew that I was fussing, that I was covering my fear, my terror, by worrying over tiny insignificant details, but it helped.

Omori stood in the centre of the room, head bowed, eyes closed. This moment could well be the last one of her life.

I looked around at the circle of traders. Everyone who had survived Okaporo had come; the rooks that had taught me my craft, and the traders that had learnt alongside me as children. No one else had lent their support. Even after a generation of living alongside them, the divide between Kagosaka and Okaporo was gaping wide. But these were my sisters, my true sisters, and we were in this together. I'd rather have fewer people that I trusted here, than hundreds that I didn't.

"Start building your mind blocks now. I need you all to focus, to concentrate. You're building a wall around Omori, not protecting yourselves. Hold hands, and be part of that wall. We have no way of knowing exactly when it will happen, so we need the block to be as strong as it can be."

I stood next to Omori, and took her hand in mine.

She pulled away from me. "No, Kioto. Stand in the circle. I don't want anyone touching me, just in case. We don't know what might happen."

I took hold of her hand again, letting the tears run freely over my face. "I'm not letting go of you."

31

MALIA

We settled ourselves on a hill just beyond the buildings which gave us a clear view of both the entrance gates, and the centre of the colony. Beyond the houses, the sea glistened under the summer sun, and the sandy beach shone just as brightly. It would be easy to believe it was gold instead of sand. Above us, gulls circled like hungry vultures.

"Do you think it will work?" I asked.

Narata looked out towards the ocean. "I don't know. I don't know what's going to happen."

"There's Tokai," I said, pointing towards the entrance.

Narata looked.

"That must be the second vessel with her."

Narata nodded.

"Do you think the first one will come? Do you think the chance to kill the last Lobayan vessel, the chance to get revenge on Tokai, will be enough?"

Narata patted my hand with her cold fingers. "We can only hope so."

I rubbed the back of my neck. "What happens if the vessels recognise each other? Because if the first vessel doesn't believe this second one is Omori, then everything is lost."

"We know that the Qathab vessels are always kept apart. We just have to hope."

Narata seemed to be far more composed than I felt. I knew I was babbling, trying to still the fluttering of my stomach with words. I rubbed my neck again and tried to focus on the scene below.

We watched as Shima walked up to Tokai. They spoke, and the conversation escalated into an argument.

"Looks like Tokai's been burning all of her bridges," Narata said.

I grabbed Narata's hand. "Here comes the other vessel."

We watched as she walked into the colony. Calm, poised. She had nothing to be afraid of. An untouchable weapon. Confident in her eminence.

She moved towards the group. I held my breath, and I swear my heart stopped in my chest. The whole world silenced, and leaned in. The vessel pushed Tokai to one side and, without speaking a single word, reached out and touched the second vessel's forehead.

133

When I described the scene to Kioto, I told her that I saw a flash, heard a pop, but I'd always question that. Something happened. Something that left me dazed, my vision patched with spots as if I'd been looking at the sun. Something that brought tears into my eyes and expelled a groan from my throat. Something happened in that moment. And I thought of all the people I loved. I thought of Omori and Kioto. I thought of Firefinch.

32

KIOTO

I fell to the floor as if someone had slammed against me. My hand slipped out of Omori's, and I scrabbled to locate it, but found only air. I landed, arms sprawled out, legs flailing. I watched as our circle of traders fell like dominoes around us.

And then the pain tore through my head. I grabbed my skull with my hands, my sight torn from me, my body unable to respond. And I thought that it was all over, that we had failed, that we were all going to die.

But then the pain began to ease. I blinked, my sight coming back to me, my senses restoring themselves.

I turned myself around and, with a heart close to exploding, dug through the tangle of bodies with shaking hands, seeing Omori's face on all of them, but not finding her. I pulled arms and legs out of the way, fought my way through hands that clawed at me, and hair that clung like seaweed. I pulled a foot aside, and she was there. Lying on her back. Unmoving. Eyes closed.

"Omori?"

She didn't respond.

I grabbed her cold, limp hand. "Omori?"

Her eyes flickered open.

33

KIOTO

A lot of coffee had been drunk, a lot of biscuits had been dipped, and a lot of bacon sandwiches had been cooked, but we all still sat, looking around at one another, waiting for someone to decide what we should do next.

I hadn't let go of Omori's hand all the way back to the rogue camp, and I still refused to let her go. I looked at her, her face tired, a bruise beginning to darken on her forehead.

"Can you still feel any of the vessels?" I asked her.

She sighed and closed her eyes. "It's just silence," she said quietly. "Like the purest silence I've ever heard."

"You don't think we could have killed them all,

do you?"

"Kioto."

I looked up at the rogue in the doorway.

"There's someone outside demanding to see you. She says her name's Tokai."

"You don't have to go out there," Dai said.

I stood up, already halfway out of the door by time I said. "No, I want to see her."

Omori trailed behind me, her hand still clasped in mine. We barely made it outside when Tokai started screaming at us.

"What on earth have you done? You've just set traders rights back by decades. This was for the good of everyone. Not to mention you could have killed us all. You've ruined everything. You have no idea what you've done."

"I did what had to be done," I said. I tried to hold my voice steady, but my jaw felt so tight that I could barely get the words out at all.

"No. No, Kioto, I was doing what had to be done."

"They weren't who you thought they were," said Omori. "They weren't fighting for trader equality."

"Of course they were. But it's all over now. They'll never trust any of us again."

"You shouldn't have trusted them," I said. "And no one should have ever trusted you."

"And what about you, Kioto? No one should come within ten metres of you. You're bad luck. Everyone you care about comes to harm. Your family, your colony, even poor Tian."

"Don't you say his name. You have no right." I clenched my fists to try and stop my hands from shaking, but the fury was pulsing through me, filling my body with heat.

"Don't I? We actually became quite intimate. I spent a lot of time in his head after we captured him. Rooting around, pulling it apart. You should go and see him, he's quite the changed man."

"You were the trader?" Omori said, stepping forward. She looked back at me. "We didn't want to worry you, Kioto, but Tian's in a state. He's had his memories torn to shreds. She really pulled him apart."

"How could you?" My hand stung as it slapped across her face. "How dare you touch him." I planted my feet firmly, but I wanted to tear her limb from limb.

"I will do the same to everyone you care about. There's more than one way to kill a vessel."

Tokai leapt at Omori, knocking her to the ground. I pulled at Tokai's shoulders, tumbling backwards with her on top of me. Her hands scratched at my face, pulled at my hair. I kicked and scrabbled back, managing to topple her off me, and pin her to the ground.

Reaching out, I found Omori's hand and held it tightly. "Don't let go!" I cried out.

And then I placed my other hand on Tokai's forehead. I grabbed hold of the first thought I found in there. Rage was easy to hold onto. It wanted to be held, to be shared. It wanted to spread. I tugged and it came easily enough. And then I began unwrapping the rest of Tokai's mind. I pulled it out through me, and pushed it into Omori, feeling it trickling away like sand in an hourglass. I pulled and pulled at everything, and I didn't stop until Tokai's mind was empty. A chasm.

I fell backwards off her, and stared at my hand.

"I can't believe what you just did," Omori whispered.

I shook my head. Neither could I. I looked at Tokai. She stared up at the sky, her gaze vacant.

"You used me," Omori whispered.

"I'm sorry," I said to the ground. It had been selfish, nothing more than instinctive revenge and pure hatred. I was sorry that I'd used Omori, but I couldn't say I was sorry for what I'd done. I felt dirty, sullied, like I'd never be clean again. But I couldn't fully say that Tokai didn't get what she deserved. I'd always been scared of rogues, but the real enemy had been amongst my own people.

"What are you going to do with her?" Omori asked.

"I'll take her to the colony. They'll look after her. And I'm going to get Tian."

"Then what?"

I turned to face the salty breeze. "Then we're going home."

34

KIOTO

I ran my hand over the sign, the letters cut deep into the slate, and painted in with gold. RAVENS GATE. Tokai had been right; they had built on the Okaporo colony, but it wasn't a casino, it was a housing estate. The walls were still crisply white, the windows still covered in protective film, the gardens still needed to mature.

I turned to Narata, her face ashen, her shoulders slumped. My heart had withered and shrunk, nothing more than a dry cherry pip in my chest. My breath caught on a sob and I fell into her arms. We cried for everything and everyone that we'd lost. Our home was gone. Our history. Our ancestors. Our roots. Everything that we were, and everything that we'd hoped to be again. Our dreams had been paved over.

Omori's arms came around me, lifting me away from Narata.

"We have each other, Kioto, that's all that matters. As long as we're together, we are home, no matter where we are."

I turned away from Ravens Gate and found the rest of the world blurred with tears. I blinked. At first, I couldn't make sense of the flashing lights. I blinked again and a hand closed tightly around my wrist.

"Kioto of Okaporo, I'm arresting you on charges of attempted murder and terrorism."

"Hold on," Dai's voice. "Charges? She's not been charged. What happened to 'on suspicion of'?"

"She's a trader. There is no suspicion."

I stumbled as I was led away, barely able to feel the ground beneath me, barely able to lift my feet. My head was smothered in fog, my sense of the world faltering. It was like being underwater. Like drowning.

"We'll get you out, Kioto," Dai called after me. "We'll do something."

As I was pushed into an auto car I looked up and spotted Omori and Tian.

"Look after him!" I cried out.

Omori may have waved back, but the scene was cut by the door sliding closed. The car hummed and began to move, taking me away from everyone.

PART TWO

ANGELINE TREVENA

35

NOLA

My eyes fluttered open and, for a moment, all I saw was bright white. It hurt. I screwed them closed again. My whole body ached and I tried to stretch out my legs, but they were stiff, and uncooperative. I wriggled, and found that my arms were equally unwilling. I opened my mouth to wail, but only a whimper escaped from my dried-out throat.

Hands gently stroked my shoulder, and their touch calmed me. I could feel. I could move. A little. I was alive.

"Good morning, sweetheart," a voice said softly. "Welcome to the world. You truly are a beautiful sight."

I opened my eyes just a crack and, through my eyelashes, I could see a face.

"That's right, open your eyes, there's nothing to be afraid of here. You're strong. You're a survivor. A miracle. And we're all so glad you're here. I need you to lie still for a moment more, Nola, don't try to move. You're still weak, your muscles need time to strengthen first. We'll just take it nice and slowly, ok?"

The hands pressed against my skin, they rubbed over it, and I could feel life moving into my limbs. Strength. Energy. I fought the urge to struggle up to standing, fought the urge to run, and dance, and jump. I felt like I'd been asleep for centuries.

I lay still and occupied myself with inspecting the face above me. The nose and mouth were covered with a white mask that shimmered as it moved. The eyes were large and dark, like they held all of the secrets in the world. I wanted those secrets. I wanted to know everything there was to know. The top of the head was covered with a hat, not a hint of hair escaped. All I had was those eyes. Those eyes that would tell me everything.

The mask sucked in as the face took a breath. "There, that's better. I've given you some additives to help to wake up this body of yours. It's brand new. It still needs to learn. Slowly now, slowly. Take my hands, and we'll get your out of your pod."

I took hold of the offered hands and gradually raised up to sitting. My head swam and I blinked the dizziness away.

"Take your time."

I curled my legs up beside me before

stretching them over the edge of the pod towards the ground.

"Let's get those muscles warmed up before you try to stand."

The hands took each leg in turn, and rubbed, hard. I could feel warmth creeping into my skin, my muscle, and bone, as if there had never been warmth there before.

"Wriggle your toes for me. Good, good. Now raise your legs from the knee. Up, up, that's it. Good girl. Do you want to try standing? I'll hold you, I won't let you fall."

I nodded. I eased myself forward and reached one foot down. The floor below was warm and ridged with rows of tiny bubbles. I shuffled further forward and placed my other foot down. I gripped hold of the arms around me as, shakily, I stood.

"Good girl, well done. See how strong you are? How about your first step? Do you think you can do that?"

I lifted a foot from the floor and moved it forward, shifting my weight onto it.

"You're a superstar. Ready for marathons, I'd say. Would you like to try it by yourself? I'll be right here, I won't let you fall."

I nodded again, quickly, in case my courage failed me. The arms released me, and I stood by myself. I raised my head, blinking in the bright whiteness of the room. I took another step, and another, and another, until my hands laid against the far wall.

"Good girl, you're doing so well."

The voice was far away now, and my knees trembled beneath me. I wanted to call the voice to me, the hands and arms to hold me, but I didn't know how. I opened my mouth and pushed a gurgle from my lips.

"Take your time," the voice said. It was coming closer. "Think of the words you want to say. You can do it. You know how. Your body is brand new, but your mind has the knowledge already."

I wasn't sure that it did. I thought, hard, my brain waking up and beginning to turn. Recharging. Ancient knowledge rousing from sleep, like I had. Stretching its legs, taking its first step.

"Help me," I whispered, surprised by the sound of my own voice. "Help me." Louder this time. "I'm scared."

The hands were on me again with the comfort of their touch.

"You don't need to be scared of anything," the voice said. "No one will ever be able to hurt you."

36

NOLA

I was woken early each morning for my lessons, even before the centre had been flooded with the artificial sunlight they lit it with, even before the projections of trees and fields covered the bare walls. I didn't know whose benefit it was for. Me, who had never been outside in my short lifetime, or the staff who regularly slipped out to take deep breaths of fresh mountain air. I could smell it on them sometimes; the scent of heather or fir, sometimes they were damp with rain, or early morning dew. I craved the outside world, longed to fill my own lungs with that air, but it was forbidden. So much here was.

I was marched up the corridor and into my classroom by two women I was only allowed to refer to as 'Nisa'. Not that I ever spoke to them, and not that they ever spoke to me.

Sometimes my teacher was Nisa Aliel, with her small waist and her tight clothes. And other times it was Nisa Tayis, who was short and dumpy, and always wore blouses buttoned up to her throat. There was also a library in the centre that I was allowed to visit. It was small and limited, the titles probably carefully selected, but I devoured the information, and had read every book numerous times.

Sometimes, like today, my teacher was nothing more than a screen. This was how I was taught history. I assumed neither Nisa Aliel or Nisa Tayis had it in them to lie to me, to feed me propaganda, and fuel me with hatred. It just made me love them more. And I played my part; watching the twisted version of trader history that they fed me, answered appropriately when they quizzed me on it afterwards.

There were a number of videos they cycled through, and I'd seen them all several times. The theme was always the same: the unjust persecution of traders. But that wasn't the part that interested me. Watching closely, the background characters held my attention. Between the fictionalised interviews with traders who had lost their whole families, and the piles of bodies, there was life, and tradition, and ceremony.

I'd asked Nisa Aliel about it once.

"Why don't we have scars like the traders in the videos?"

"Because that's an outdated practice. We no longer scar our children here in Qathab."

"Why not?"

"Because it's barbaric."

"But it's traditional."

"Just because something's traditional doesn't mean it's right."

"Are there any traders that still wear the traditional scars?"

Nisa Aliel had thought for a moment. I couldn't tell whether she was trying to remember, or just deciding what she was going to tell me.

"Yes," she'd said at last. "Yes, there are."

"Where?"

"Not in Qathab. That's all you need to know."

And then she'd patted my arm and changed the subject. Far from shutting down the conversation, her reluctance merely fuelled my curiosity. I needed to know who these traders were that still practised in the traditional way.

The first time Nisa Aliel had taken me outside I had stood, for a moment, overwhelmed by the enormity of it, by the cacophony of sounds and smells that came rushing at me. It had appeared unconquerable, and intimidating, and terrifying. I had run back inside and cowered, crying, in my room.

Today was going to be different. Today I had decided to be brave.

Nisa Aliel took hold of my hand and smiled down at me. Her smile was so warm, so honest, her eyes creasing up and flashing. "You ready?"

I nodded.

"I won't let go of you, ok? We rushed it last time, that was my fault, not yours. Whatever you feel, that's real, and legitimate. Never apologise for your feelings, ok?"

I nodded again.

She passed her ID over the door lock, and it clicked open. Through the tiny crack in the door I could smell and hear the world beyond. I breathed it in deeply. Some of the smells settled on my tongue, and I hungered for more.

"When you're ready," Nisa Aliel said softly, "just push the door open. Or, we can just stand here, you don't have to go outside today. Not if you don't want to. We'll take it nice and slowly."

With the option of going no further, my confidence began to waver. I'd woken up completely determined, but I hadn't realised that not going outside was going to be an option. I craved the wonder of the world as much as I craved the sanctuary of the centre.

I slipped my hand free of Nisa Aliel's grip, and braced myself. I took a deep breath and propelled my legs, full pelt, out of the door. I ran, crashing through bushes, slipping on damp grass, ducking under low branches, and startling a crow into the air. I ran until my chest ached, until my heartbeat thumped in my head, until my knees burnt and their strength wavered. And then I dropped to the ground, flattening a patch of daffodils. I closed my eyes, and let the sun warm my skin.

My heart pounded, but not from fear this time. The world, so full of wonderful things, so full of discoveries and treasures, had embraced me, and I embraced it back. This was where I was meant to be.

37

NOLA

I woke to voices outside my room. They argued in harsh whispers, their breathy words sliding under my door like secret notes.

"She's too curious about the old ways. We've done our best to discourage her, but the questions keep coming."

"It's in her blood, it's harmless. No one here will indulge her with answers."

"If it's an issue with the DNA, we could terminate and try again."

"Try again? You know what's happened to any subsequent test subjects. Catastrophic brain anomalies. I've seen some things I never want to see again."

"So the destruction was complete?"

"The laboratories were devastated."

"And Nola? How did she survive?"

The question was left unanswered for some time.

"She was made using a different formula."

"What formula?"

"The blood of the betrayal."

"That blood was forbidden. It was ordered that it all be destroyed."

"And if I hadn't, then we would have nothing."

"Do you think a vessel brimming with traitor blood is better? Who was the maternal donor?"

"An ancient source. Unknown."

"An ancient Lobayan source?" The silence hung in the air like raised daggers. "Then you have betrayed us all."

"I added in a third donor, a strong Qathab bloodline. I thought that by using a different DNA combination we could solve the proximity issue. This research is so slow going because we can only ever have one vessel in a centre at a time. It's agonising. And what we have in there is a vessel, the only vessel, and she survived the devastation because her blood was different to all the others."

I rolled over to better hear the voices, and sent an avalanche of books sliding off my bed. I froze, holding my breath. The voices silenced, listening.

After a long wait, they spoke again. "And the thoughts, the history in her blood?"

"They're building blocks, raw materials. What we teach her in the centre is what matters. Her education. Which is going to plan. Did you see Nisa

Aliel's report from today? She's becoming independent, courageous, facing her fears. I think it's time to begin her training."

"I'm not sure that independence is necessarily something to be encouraged. We'll assess her tomorrow. But your betrayal will not be forgotten. Nor will it be forgiven."

38

NOLA

"What am I?" I asked.

"What?" Nisa Irrin, my ever-present assessor, looked up from her screen for a second and eyed me over the top of her glasses. Her eyes returned to the green glow in front of her.

"What am I?" I asked again.

"You're a company asset," she replied, without looking up this time.

"She's a child." Nisa Aliel had argued her way into the room just before my assessment began.

Nisa Irrin looked up at me. "Yes," she said. "Physically, you are a child. Emotionally, that's a more difficult thing to determine. But your purpose, your destiny, is far more than that. And your importance and value is immeasurable. Does that answer your question?"

I shrugged and looked over at Nisa Aliel.

"How is she supposed to understand that?" she asked, reflecting my own thoughts.

Nisa Irrin looked back at her screen. "She'll understand what she wants to. It's not my job to cradle her emotional ego."

"And what about her sense of self? Her sense of her place in the world?"

"That is of no importance."

"How is that of no importance?"

"I mean, it has no bearing on this assessment. Nisa Aliel, you are present on my kindness. If you cannot contain yourself, I will have you removed."

"Please," I said. "I want her here."

Nisa Irrin sighed deeply. Leaning forward across the table, she pressed pads onto my forehead. "Hands out," she said.

I offered my hands to her, and pads were pressed onto the tips of each of my fingers.

"I'm going to show you some images, some short video clips, and play you some audio. I don't need you to say anything, simply think through your reactions and thoughts to each of them. The pads will read your mental and physical output to assess your responses. Understand?"

I nodded.

To start with, each clip or image was familiar to me; taken from the videos I'd been shown since I woke up. They called it 'birthed', but, from what I'd learnt about birth, it was nothing of the kind. Perhaps 'created' would be a more appropriate word. Or 'manufactured' even.

After a while, the images changed. They became more bloody, more violent, more graphic. My stomach churned and I felt the heat of fury rise up from deep in my stomach. But it wasn't the fury they wanted me to feel, fury against the rest of the world, it was fury that they were doing this to me. That they were brainwashing me to hate. Turning me into a product of rage. A weapon. I knew what I was. And I knew that I would do everything I could not to become what they wanted me to.

39

NOLA

"Put your hand on her forehead."

I did as I was told, instinctively laying my other hand against the girl's stomach.

"No." My second hand was slapped away. "Just use one hand."

I screwed my fingers into a fist. I closed my eyes, silently reciting as much of the Dedication as I could remember. They wouldn't stop me from doing that.

"Just feel your way into her mind, gently. Now I want you to have a look around, just get a feel for what it's like in there. Don't attempt to extract anything, once you start pulling you could unravel everything. Just wander around in there, nose about, poke at things. Just until you feel comfortable. You'll have to feel comfortable with being inside someone else's mind."

"How can anyone ever feel comfortable with that?" I asked.

"You'll have to find a way, Nola."

I broke the connection, stepping away from the subject. "It's not right," I said. "Poking around in there. Not without permission."

"You're a vessel, you don't need permission, and we certainly won't be training you to ask for it."

"Maybe someone else should do my training. Maybe in one of the colonies—"

The slap stung my cheek and brought tears to my eyes. I raised my hand to my face and found the skin burning hot and already rising in welts. Without thinking I reached out and grabbed the hand that had struck me. I pushed a thought in, and with it I sent pain and hurt and sadness.

"Yes!" Nisa Irrin called from across the room. "Yes, Nola. Push that thought into her."

I stumbled backwards staring at my own hand in horror. I looked at the woman, her hand repeatedly slapping her own face.

Nisa Irrin applauded.

"What have I done?" I whispered. As I ran from the room, I collided with a trolley and I toppled with it, spilling its contents onto the floor.

I was still curled up on my bed when a sharp knock rattled my door. I rolled over and faced the wall.

The door opened and footsteps entered. The bed dipped with the weight of someone sitting down, and a hand landed on my hip.

"How are you feeling?" Nisa Tayis asked. "I hear you had a bit of a shock, so I asked if I could check on you."

I shrugged.

"Come on, Nola. We all get angry, and we all get overwhelmed with emotion. We're only human. You can't blame yourself."

I rolled over and looked up at her. "But I'm not, am I? I'm not human. Not really."

"Oh, darling." She pulled me up into her thick arms and smothered me into her chest. "Of course you are, and don't let anyone ever tell you any different."

I nodded my agreement, but I didn't feel it. Nisa Irrin was right: I was an asset. A product. And I was becoming everything they'd created me to be.

"I've been given permission to give you a little treat, but you'll have to hurry up before it gets too late."

Curiosity lifted me from the bed, and tied my shoes onto my feet. I followed Nisa Tayis up the corridor with my head bowed. I could feel eyes on me, and the few people we passed gave me a wide berth. I had become something to fear.

Nisa Tayis opened a door, and I smelt the outside world. But it was different. It was cooler, and the scents had shifted into something new. Something heavier, more musky.

I stepped out of the door into the world as I'd never seen it before. The sky was a deep purple above me, freckled with emerging stars, and a line of rose gold lay along the horizon, bathing the landscape in a blush.

"What is this?" I whispered, fearful that any loud noise might scare it all away.

"This is sunset," Nisa Tayis replied softly. "The end of the day."

"Dusk," I whispered.

"That's right. The world is a different place after dark."

"It's like magic."

"Look, Nola, look." Nisa Tayis pointed to a patch of heather a little way from us.

I squinted into the half light and saw several pairs of black eyes looking back at me.

"Rabbits," I said, completely awed by their twitching noses and long ears that swivelled to the sound of my voice. They were the first real animals I'd ever seen.

"They're quite tame," Nisa Tayis said. "The staff feed them scraps and, if you're patient, some of them will take food right from your hand."

"Could I feed them?" My body trembled at the idea.

"Not tonight. Maybe another time. They'll have to learn to trust you."

Somewhere in the distance a woman screamed, and I grabbed Nisa Tayis' hand. Her body stiffened at my touch.

She turned to me with a tight smile. "Just a fox, Nola. You have nothing to be scared of."

"But I am scared," I said.

"New things are always scary."

"Am I evil?"

Nisa Tayis crouched down and looked me straight in the eye. "No. You are not. You are a precious child with a huge amount of responsibility on your shoulders. Responsibility you shouldn't have to carry. But that's the way it is. You are who you are, and that's never going to change. But you can decide what to do with it. You can decide how to use it."

I looked down at my hands. "I'll never do that out of anger again."

Nisa Tayis pushed my hair back from my face. "We can never know what might happen to us, or how we might react when it does. What will happen will happen. You only have to do your best."

"My best at what? What Nisa Irrin wants me to do? Or what I feel in my heart?"

40

NOLA

I settled down in the hard chair in front of the screen. I had hoped to see Nisa Tayis waiting for me, waiting to take me back outside, but I'd have to wait to see the world again.

Although I wasn't alone with the screen today. Nisa Irrin was sitting next to me.

"We're going to watch a slightly different video today," she said. "A part of your story that we haven't talked about yet. We call it the 'devastation', and it happened just before you were birthed. You were the only survivor. It is a deeply held trader belief, a sacred belief, that you do not betray your fellow traders. As you are well aware, we have been persecuted by every other group throughout history, and so, it is absolutely forbidden to betray your own people. It is the worst kind of treachery, and will be met with swift and severe retribution. We stand as one, Nola, and if someone hurts one of us, they hurt us all." She pressed her forefinger and thumb together and an image flicked up onto the screen.

It was a picture of the centre, I recognised the building with the mountains behind. Standing in the foreground was Nisa Irrin and another woman.

"This is the vessel who came before you." She clicked her fingers again and the picture showed a similar scene, but the woman next to Nisa Irrin was different. "And the vessel who came before her." She cycled through similar pictures. "A whole line of vessels, birthed just like you were, here at Eayan Aljibal. These are your ancestors."

"Are they buried here?" I asked.

"No. They were destroyed in the devastation. Let me explain. There are four other centres, just like this one. At Qatkha, Jiddir, Alja, and Harkha, and there has been a line of vessels birthed at each of them. They are also your ancestors, you are all one. These women were special, just like you are. And one act destroyed them all, an act of the worst kind of treachery. Carried out by a fellow trader."

A picture of a trader appeared on the screen. She wasn't looking at the camera, she wasn't posing, she was walking, caught mid-stride, completely unaware that her picture had been taken. Nisa Irrin cycled through several more similar shots of her. I leaned forward and inspected her closely.

"I want you to remember this face. You need to be able to recognise it if you ever come across it. This is the face of a traitor to all of our people. Her name is Kioto of Okaporo."

"Okaporo," I whispered.

"You know your history then. Yes, the colony that was massacred. Kioto was one of the few survivors. A group of young traders were visiting another colony with their rooks. They are all that remains of the Okaporo people. They are a people of betrayal, and it is our duty to meet that betrayal with retribution. We must end the Okaporo line, and destroy all of its blood."

I leaned closer to the screen, searching Kioto's face for the pain of her past.

"What did she do?" I asked.

"She caused the devastation. She tricked two of your ancestors into coming together, into touching one another. You've learnt about the importance of that, haven't you?"

I looked down at my hands and nodded.

"That touch swept through the heads of all vessels. It killed them all instantly. They shared DNA, Nola, they were all one in the same. There were four other vessels in stasis, just like you were, at the time of the devastation. You were the only survivor."

"Why?"

"Because your blood is different. Your DNA isn't the same. And because you're strong, Nola, you've proven that. You're truly formidable."

"So, I'm the last vessel?"

"There was one other that survived the devastation." A new image was brought up on the screen. A young trader. Another image of her. And one of her with Kioto.

"Who is she?"

"This is Omori. Kioto's sister, and the last Lobayan vessel. You need to remember her face too. Make sure you can recognise it. See how she doesn't wear trader scars like Kioto does."

"I see."

"These two traders are traitors to all of our people. It is your purpose to carry out the retribution due to them. It is your duty to kill them."

"I have to..." I didn't finish the sentence.

"They are cunning, and clever, and false. And you need to know, Nola, your DNA comes from the same bloodline. You have the same father. Kioto and Omori are your half sisters."

41

OMORI

I blinked as the first spits of rain landed on my skin. The sea breeze blew them inland, tainting them with salt. The wind always blew inland, battering the houses that dared to stand directly in its gaze. Some days it felt like it was personal, a rebuffal meant just for me. And it always felt justified. Always.

I closed my eyes as the rain grew heavier, and I let it soak me before I turned and went inside.

"Why do you do this?" Tian asked, wrapping me with one of the towels he had started stacking next to the door.

"It's just rain," I said. "It's nothing."

"Nothing in comparison, eh? You have to stop punishing yourself."

"It's been almost two years, Tian. And I've done nothing."

"You've done lots. You've reclaimed Okaporo. When Kioto gets released, she'll be able to come home. That's the one thing she's always wanted."

I shrugged. "Actually Dai reclaimed Okaporo for us. He's the government's golden boy now." I smirked. "Much to his displeasure, of course."

Tian waved a dismissive hand at me. "He was given Okaporo. The government were glad to offload it."

"Well, who thought a housing estate on an old colony would ever work? Of course no one wanted to live here."

"And the government were forced to buy every single house from the construction company. After all, they had commissioned the build."

"I guess the past isn't as easy to erase as they thought it would be."

"Dai may have reclaimed the land, but you've built Okaporo to what it is now. You've made a sister relationship with Iwoyo and brought men into the colony. And in just a few weeks' time, we'll see the arrival of the first of a brand new Okaporo generation. Living free in their true home."

I ran my hand over the swell of my stomach, delighting at the small barrage of kicks that followed.

"And Kioto will become an auntie. Just imagine that."

Tian laughed. "And she had thought that she was all alone in the world."

I nodded, his words cutting deeply through me. "And now she is again."

Tian grabbed my hand and squeezed it tightly. "No, that's not what I meant. Look at what she'll come home to."

I shook my head. "If she ever comes home. They're making an example of her. Now that we're at war with Qathab, they can't be seen to be showing any leniency."

"Dai will sort it out. She's a hero, and she should be recognised as such."

"Dai isn't the miracle worker you think he is. He's a figurehead, the face of a government PR campaign. They needed a hero, and they didn't want that hero to be a trader."

Tian nodded slowly, his eyes beginning to glaze over. He was disappearing into himself again. I sat him down by the window, and he turned to watch the waves beating against the cliffs. He seemed happy enough in those moments, and they'd become less frequent over the last couple of years. I liked to think that his brain was mending itself, filling in the gaps that Tokai left.

I turned as the front door opened. Jodo bowed through the gap, his hulk filling the frame. He brought with him the smell of animals, of damp straw, of food pellets and smoke. I pressed my face into his jacket and breathed in the scent of him. His arms closed around me like a fortress.

"You're wet," he said. "Have you been standing out in the rain again?"

"I'm fine."

"It's not just you I have to look after now." He crouched and placed his face against my belly. "Hey little guy, are you alright in there?"

I laughed and pushed him gently away.

"You should get changed," he said. "And dry your hair before you get ill. Our little man needs you to be healthy." Jodo glanced over at Tian. "How's he doing today?"

I nodded. "Good, yeah. Still as optimistic as ever. And this is the first time he's drifted off in several days."

"Maybe it's time we settled him into his own house. There are plenty to choose from. We could use the extra space once the baby comes."

"No. I promised Kioto I'd look after him."

"You'll still be looking after him. The independence will do him good."

"No, Jodo. Please don't ask me again."

He shrugged. "Just a suggestion. He can stay. Whatever makes you happy." He kissed me with dry, chafed lips. "As long as he doesn't mind a screaming baby."

I grinned. "Maybe I'll move out then."

"Don't you dare." He loped off towards the bedroom calling "I'd chain you to the bed first" over his shoulder.

42

NOLA

Nisa Tayis had taught me the names of everything outside. The plants, the bugs, the trees, the flowers, even the names of the clouds. She'd pointed out the mountain peaks, and the streams, and given a name to each of them, and I'd memorised them all, holding them close to me like treasures.

There was power in the names of things, and it gave me a sense of ownership over the world. It made it familiar, like an old friend, or like family. Like a house I was welcome to walk into without knocking.

I had brought bread from my lunch plate, hidden in my pocket. I crumbled it between my fingers and tossed it across the grass, naming each of the birds as they came.

I lay back on the ground and watched the sky begin to darken, the first stars fighting for recognition in an expanse that still held onto the light. The strongest ones sparkled and winked, defiant of the sun that sought to extinguish them with its own glow.

The ground beneath me began to cool, and a breeze rippled my skin into goosebumps. I closed my eyes and listened to the world settle down for the night, tuck itself into bed. But another world was only now waking up, with its bright eyes that glowed like luminescent pools, and ears that heard sounds far beyond the reaches of my own senses.

I rolled onto my stomach and looked over to where Nisa Tayis puffed on a cigarette, the end of it glowing like a beacon of guilt. She wasn't supposed to smoke in front of me, she'd told me so, but she trusted me. And that trust was something I was about to betray.

I tossed more food across the grass, and drew my secret treasure from my other pocket. The blade glinted in the last rays of sunlight, ominously announcing its intent like a heliograph winking out Morse code. It was a scalpel, taken from the trolley I'd toppled in the laboratory. I hadn't taken it for any reason, for any particular purpose. It had simply been there, and I had been so scared. Perhaps I'd had a fleeting thought of ending my own life.

The rabbits truly were tame, and happily ate crumbs from my fingers. I threw another glance towards Nisa Tayis whose face was now bathed in the greenish light of a small screen that floated before her.

I reached out and stroked one of the animals, smoothing down its warm fur. I gripped it around the neck, pushing the fur aside, and placing my thumb against its skin. I willed it to be quiet, pushed in the thought to submit, and it went limp in my hand.

I pressed the scalpel into its flesh, driving it deep, and pulling it around the creature's neck. The rabbit made no movement to try and save its life. Blood gushed over the ground, and I launched myself backwards away from the growing pool.

I reached out and grabbed the rabbit, moving further away from the blood. Just beyond the heather, a large arrow of rock had pushed up through the grass, and I placed the rabbit on the flattest section that I could find. I removed its feet and its head, and then grabbed the scruff at the back of its neck. I sliced across it, and turned the scalpel to draw it the length of the animal's back. The skin came away far easier than I expected it to; the actual act was so different to simply reading about it. It wasn't a perfect job, but it was a good chunk of pelt. I lay the skinned rabbit out on the rock. The fox would find it.

At the stream, I washed the piece of fur, watching as the water flowed with streaks of red.

Back in my bedroom, I bid goodnight to Nisa Tayis and listened as her footsteps led her away up the corridor.

Dropping to my knees, I eased the bottom panel out of my bedside table and pulled out the items I'd hidden in there. A bowl stolen from the kitchen, a pebble taken from the stream, heather torn from the ground. I pulled the damp rabbit pelt from my pocket and laid it with the other items. It was everything I needed to be a proper trader. There was just one more thing to do.

I stood and crossed to the basin in the far corner of my room. I looked in the mirror and inspected my right eye, the smooth, unblemished skin around it. I'd begged an eye liner pencil from Nisa Aliel. She'd been amused by the request, and had spent some time showing me all the items in her make up bag, explaining methods for using each of them. But I hadn't been interested in concealer or lipstick.

I drew three black lines above my eye, and three below. I took a deep breath, and lifted the scalpel to my face.

43

OMORI

Whenever Dai came to Okaporo it was an event. His car had barely pulled into Ravens Gate before it was swarmed by people. He pretended to find it annoying, shooing them away as he pushed his way through them, but I knew he secretly enjoyed the attention. Who didn't like to arrive somewhere and know, instantly, that they have been terribly missed?

I stood at my front door and watched the usual pandemonium with a smile.

Dai burst out of the crowd of greeters and raised his eyes to me. He smiled warmly and I returned his enthusiastic wave.

He peeled a child from his leg and jogged over to where I was standing.

"Hello Mumma," he said. "How are the ankles? Swollen like balloons?"

"You always say the sweetest things."

He glanced over his shoulder. "Quick, let me in before I get mobbed again."

I turned and went inside, Dai close behind me. "It must be hard being such an adored celebrity."

Dai dropped into a chair. "It's a hardship. How's everything here?"

I eased myself onto the sofa and hefted my heavy legs up onto the cushions.

"Fine. Ticking along."

"How's Tian?"

"Fine. Getting better, I think. How's the war going?"

Dai shrugged. "How do wars ever go? Futile, devastating, wasteful."

"Any news on Kioto? Have you managed to see her yet?"

"Not yet." He grinned. "But I have a visit booked for tomorrow." He jiggled in his seat like an excited child. "The order only just came through, so I wanted to come and tell you straight away. In person."

I stared at him, hardly able to believe it. "What will you say to her?"

"Whatever you want me to. I'm your proxy. Give me any messages you want. I mean, do you want me to tell her about Okaporo? About..." He gestured towards my stomach as if it were a large boil he was trying to avoid mentioning.

"Yes, why wouldn't you? Yes, tell her

everything. Tell her everything she'll be coming home to."

"It's a visit, not her release."

"Your job is to make sure she's remaining positive. If she gives up, that place will kill her. You make sure to get her smiling."

He leaned back in the chair, his face plastered with a wide grin. "With my sparkling charisma, that shouldn't be hard."

"I dunno… she does hate you."

He waved a hand at me. "Rubbish, she loves me."

"And how are things with you? How's the governmental life treating you?"

He rolled his half-lidded eyes and groaned. "Everything just moves so slowly. Meetings and meetings and meetings. I am not joking, I was once in a three-day meeting. We went home at the end of each day, and in the morning, we picked up where we left off. Honestly, I think it might actually send me to the nuthouse."

"I'm sure the pay packet makes up for it though."

"It's the one thing that gets me through. Is business here any better?"

I shook my head. "I can't remember the last time anyone did an extraction. No one wants traders poking around in their heads anymore. But, we're self sufficient. The farm's well established, and the crops are growing. I wish the orchard was a little more mature, but we're still a small colony, so I'm happy that there's plenty to go round. Some of the men have taken jobs in the city, so I think we'll manage to get through the winter alright."

"You've done really good work here."

"It's all Narata's doing, I'm just her mouthpiece really."

"And how is she finding it being a brood mother again?"

"Absolutely relishing it. Honestly, you'd hardly know so many years had passed since she was last in charge here. She picked it back up as if she'd never stopped."

He nodded, his face becoming serious. "I'm sorry I couldn't get you in to see her."

I rubbed my stomach. "Probably not the best thing right now, for me to travel all the way up to Aojima and enter a high security prison."

He nodded again. "I wish I could do more. But I'm not a diplomat, I don't have any real sway. It's more PR and photo shoots." He snorted. "Who'd have ever thought I would be a pin-up." He gestured to his creased, weathered face.

"I don't know... To a certain type of lady..."

"Old, you mean." He laughed. "You don't have to be polite. I've lived the life I wanted to, and it shows. I have no regrets about that." He stood up. "I ought to get going. I have to be back in Aojima in a few hours."

"More meetings?"

"You know it. I'll pop in on Malia and Firefinch first. Has she received her freedom papers and citizen ID yet?"

"Not as far as I know."

"I'll make some noises, see if I can hurry it along a bit. She deserves to be a free woman."

"I wonder what she'll do with it."

"Marry that boy first, I hope."

I smiled bitterly. "Life's moving on, isn't it?"

Dai patted my shoulder. "We'll get her out. Don't give up on her."

"I won't. I'll never give up."

44

NOLA

I stood in the corridor and stared Nisa Irrin in the face. I refused to act humble or apologetic. I wasn't sorry for what I'd done.

Nisa Irrin held my blood-stained pillow in her hands.

It didn't take them long to find my hidden altar items. I knew that they'd find them, I didn't even care that much. For one night I'd been a proper trader; true to my roots, and honouring my ancestors. But they couldn't undo the scars. I'd wear them for life, a constant reminder of what I truly was.

There would be questions, a lot of questions. How did I get hold of a scalpel, how did I manage to skin a rabbit without anyone knowing? I felt bad for

Nisa Tayis, but she had been neglectful in her duties. That wasn't my fault. Although the knot in my stomach knew that I'd betrayed her trust, a trust that I'd never win back.

"Why did you do this?" Nisa Irrin demanded. There was a quiver in her voice and I realised that she felt personally affronted by this.

I frowned at her.

She grabbed hold of my wrist, wrenching my arm sideways. I stumbled. "Why did you do this?" she asked again. "You've ruined your face forever. And this—" She gestured to where my altar items had been thrown on the floor. "Why would you act with such disregard for everything we've taught you? Everything we've done for you?" She clamped her hand over her mouth as a sob escaped.

"Because this is who I am," I said. "And this is who I want to be."

"I knew it." She bent down so that her face was level with mine. "Your blood is bad." She straightened. "Patch her up. If you care to." She marched away down the corridor.

I was taken the other way, and sat in a chair in one of the medical rooms.

"Nola." I knew that voice. It was the first voice I had ever heard. "What have you done to yourself?"

The woman walked around to the front of me, only her familiar eyes visible between her hat and her mask.

"It's you," I said.

She nodded. "Yes. I was here at your birthing."

"Did you make me?"

She nodded.

"What's your name?"

She lowered her mask and smiled. "You can call me Nisa Mara."

"Does it mean you're my mother?"

She shook her head. "No, I'm not your mother. You do carry a tiny slice of my DNA though." She shook her head. "But it's a tiny, tiny bit. Your mother… your mother is unknown."

"And my father is the same as Kioto and Omori."

She flinched at the sound of their names. "You should refer to them as 'the betrayers'." She set about cleaning the scars that surrounded my eye. "Why did you do this, Nola? You must have known it would make Nisa Irrin angry."

"It made her sad more than anything. Like I'd really hurt her. Why would she feel like that? It wasn't personal."

"Everything about this centre is personal to Nisa Irrin. Her grandmother established it. The centre is everything to her. Her identity even. By doing this you've insulted her, her late mother, and her late grandmother. Qathab holds family honour in very, very high regard."

"This is who I am. Just like she wants to honour her family, I want to honour mine."

"But this isn't who you are supposed to be."

"Who I was 'designed' to be, you mean."

Nisa Mara nodded slowly. "I'm sorry, Nola."

"For what? Bringing me into this? Creating me to be at odds with myself? At odds with everything?" I pushed her hand away. "There's no need to fix me, I'm perfect now. You used the wrong blood, Nisa Mara, if you'd wanted me to become what I'm meant to become."

"And what is that?"

"A weapon. A weapon fuelled with hate."

"Is that what you think? You're not a weapon, Nola. You're hope. You're the only hope that we have."

"This isn't hope. This is... I don't even know what this is. But it's perverse, and it's cruel."

Nisa Mara nodded, her eyes filling with tears. "All I've ever wanted was children of my own. But I can't have any. My body won't carry them. I had eight miscarriages before I started working here, and another two since. I became an embryologist to help women who couldn't have children naturally, years before I ever tried for my own. Ironically, I became one of the women I was trying to help. Maybe, somehow, my body already knew. I never intended to be doing this." She gestured to the room around us. "I excelled in the field and I was asked to join the programme here. It was an amazing opportunity." She sighed. "I have birthed five vessels here, including you. I have attempted many more times, but they have all ended in failure. Yet, I will never be a mother, Nola. I will never hold a baby of my own in my arms. And so, I know about wanting to be something, and the world forcing you to be something else."

I nodded slowly.

"But I learnt a few things from it," she

continued. "You have to look to the future, Nola. Don't turn around and obsess over the past, over things that have been, or over things that might have been. The past is gone. You need to look forward, to take what you've been given and decide what to do with it."

"What should I do with this?" I held my hands out.

"I can't decide that for you. And you mustn't let anyone else make that decision. It's yours to make. Yours alone. Give me your hand."

I held it out to her. She turned it over and ran her thumb over the back of my wrist. "Here," she said, pressing her thumb against my skin. "You're fitted with a tracker. You're a valuable asset, and they don't want to lose you. They will always come looking for you, no matter where you go. So always be unexpected. They know you, they made you, and if you go where they expect you to, they'll catch you. Do you understand?" She picked up a scalpel from the trolley next to her. "Like I said, it's all about making choices. You don't always know if they're the right ones, and they all have consequences. Remember that. No decision happens without an impact on everything else."

She pressed a patch against my skin, and anaesthetic oozed from its bed of tiny needles. After a moment, she made a small incision in my arm and eased out a tiny piece of metal. She offered it to me on the end of the blade.

"That's my choice," she said. "The next one is yours."

45

OMORI

I'd been pacing the floor for almost an hour now. Dai had called when he'd reached the prison, and I was waiting for him to call back.

I glanced at Tian who looked as anxious as I felt. He was sat in the chair, legs curled underneath him, chewing his fingernails down to the bone.

I stopped, and only then realised how much my back was aching. I kneaded my fingers into the flesh and eased myself down onto the sofa. I rested my head back and stared at the ceiling.

"I can't do this anymore,"

I heard Tian rise out of the chair. "Are you alright? Can I get you anything?"

"Stop fussing, it's just backache. I just can't stand this waiting. I feel like I've been waiting for years."

"I know what you mean."

I looked up at him. "Do you think she'll ever get to come home?"

Tian swept over to me and took my hands in his. "Of course, of course she will. How could she not? She has a home to come back to now. And a sister. And how could she not come back when she has a nephew to love?" He placed his hand on my belly.

"And you," I said. "She has you to come back to as well."

He turned away, his face flushing. "Maybe."

"You've put your life on hold waiting for her."

"No, I haven't."

"You know you have."

My phone buzzed on the coffee table, and I reached out, knocking it to the floor. Tian jumped up and retrieved it, thrusting it towards me. My fingers fumbled again, and it almost slipped from my grasp.

"How is she?" I asked, dispensing with any kind of needless greeting.

"Do you want me to tell you the truth?" Dai asked.

"Yes. Please. I need to know."

"She's broken. Physically and emotionally. She's had a tough time of it. Broken fingers that have never properly healed, scars, cuts, bruises. Her hair has been hacked off, although she tells me they do it to cut down on head lice or something. She's folded in on herself, she was barely there at all when I arrived."

"Did you tell her everything? Did you tell her about Okaporo?"

"Well, you did tell me to put a smile on her face. Despite everything, I saw the old, familiar Kioto. I saw the sea in her eyes again."

"I wonder how soon they'll beat it out of her." My voice cracked, tears pushing their way up my throat.

"I will get her out of there," said Dai. "I have to. I'll find a way, I promise." The line went dead.

I looked up at Tian's expectant face. "She's doing really well," I lied. "Dai says she's staying positive, and the news about this place made her even more determined to get out of there. Dai's going to work on it, too."

Tian beamed and nodded.

"I'm so tired after all that pacing," I said. "I'm going for a nap."

"Ok. I might go for a walk. Maybe drop in on Malia and Firefinch."

I was relieved for the empty house, because I had barely made it through the bedroom door when the tears came with such force that I howled and wailed like the wind.

46

NOLA

Walking out of the centre was easy. They had no protection, no safeguards in place, because they never expected a vessel to leave. They never expected a vessel to rebel. A simple touch to the hand, and I could control anyone.

I walked straight out of the front door, at the precise time Nisa Mara had advised me to, when most of the staff were at lunch. I even turned and waved at the camera as I went. I forced myself to keep a steady pace down the road, until I was out of sight. I wanted them to know that they didn't scare me, because I knew they couldn't stop me. Only then did I run.

I left the road and crashed through forest, stumbling over roots and rocks, forcing my way through bushes that scratched, and tore, and tangled. The mountain sloped steeply here, and I was propelled downwards, grabbing hold of trees to slow my tumble, trees that whipped, and shredded my hands as they pulled their branches free of my grip. This world had become my enemy, intent on destroying me. Or perhaps, it saw the need to protect itself from me.

I finally broke free of the trees and found myself running through golden pastures of corn that rippled as I passed through. I stopped, and looked back up at the mountains. They seemed so far away all of a sudden, their peaks shrouded in clouds.

I dropped to my knees, suddenly weak with exhaustion. The ground was warm under the sun, and I lay down and looked up at the sky. I closed my eyes, my chest still heaving for breath. And then I heard it. Laughter. A child laughing. I rolled over onto my stomach and held my breath, listening, waiting for it to come again. And then I was up, following the sound of it.

I'd never seen another child before. And I'd never seen a boy. There were only women in the centre. He was playing with a young dog; holding a stick in the air, so that the dog had to jump for it. Just before the animal's jaws claimed their prize, he pulled it out of reach.

I ached with loneliness, and my body tingled at the thought of having another child to talk to. Someone to play with. Someone the same age as me. To just be a normal kid for the first time in my life.

I stepped out of the tall corn, and the boy froze. The dog growled. The boy's eyes jumped from me to the mountains, and back again.

"Where did you come from?" he asked.

"The field."

"Did you come from the mountains?"

I shook my head.

The boy backed away. "You're from the mountains."

"Can I play with you?"

The boy backed further away. He bent and took hold of the dog's collar.

In a few strides I closed the gap between us and took hold of the boy's hand. I pushed a thought into his head. It slid in so easily, nestling into his mind like it had always been there. I could have put any thought I wanted in there. Made him do anything. Simply instructed him to stop breathing. Like it or not, I was a weapon. I would never just be a normal kid.

The boy released his grip on the dog, and it ran off, yelping as it went.

"Do you want to play?" he asked me.

I shook my head. "No, thank you."

The boy blinked, his face screwed up in confusion, as if he'd just woken up and wasn't sure where he was.

"I'm sorry," I said, and walked back into the field.

47

NOLA

I looked up as a fighter jet tore across the purple sky. It was the first sign I'd seen that we were a country at war. They hadn't taught me very much about politics, beyond what the government had done to persecute traders, but I knew that, these days, war was more about diplomacy, long meetings, and sanctions than actual fighting. Besides, Kioto had wiped out Qathab's true army, and its one last hope, me, was running away.

I was following the road, but staying off it as much as I could. I ran in large arcs through woodland and farmland, doubling back to the road time and time again to check that I hadn't lost it completely.

But now it was getting dark, and a light rain

was beginning to fall. I needed to find shelter, or find a different way to travel.

I made my way back towards the road, stopping when I met tarmac. I looked left and right. There were no vehicles here. The main road had been busy. This one was narrower. For a second, I panicked, thinking I'd managed to lose the road altogether.

I bunched my fists against my chest. "No," I said aloud. "This road must join the main road. You're not lost. This road is just in your way."

I stepped onto it, the surface shining in the last of the sunlight.

I didn't hear the car behind me, I only heard the tires slip on the wet road as the auto brakes stopped it inches from me.

I spun around and stared at the face of the terrified man inside. The door slowly opened, and he stepped halfway out.

"Are you ok?" His voice trembled.

I nodded, realising that I was shaking too.

"I just… I just couldn't see you."

"It was my fault. But I'm fine."

"What are you doing walking down the middle of the road in the dark? Where are your parents?"

"I don't have any."

"Can I give you a lift somewhere?"

I looked up at the darkening sky, and the rain soaked my face. I walked towards the car, and the door slid open for me. I climbed inside. It was warm, and comfortable. The man sat back inside and both doors slid closed.

"Where are you going?"

"I'm going to find my sisters. They're in Lobaya."

"Lobaya? You can't walk all the way to Lobaya. Even if you did, we're at war, they're not going to let you stroll over the border. Why are your sisters in Lobaya?"

I shrugged. "It's where they live."

"I'll take you to the next town," he said with a decisive nod. "That's where I live. I can take you to the police station, they'll be able to help you get back home."

The car hummed and pulled away.

"Please don't take me to the police," I said. "I can't go back."

"You're just a child. If you've run away from home... It's not safe for you to be alone out here."

"You don't need to worry about me. No one can hurt me."

"I have children of my own. I'd like to think that, if anyone ever found them lost, they'd do the right thing."

"I'm not lost. Please, I just need to get to my sisters. If you could take me to Harkha I can make my own way from there."

The man shook his head vigorously. "Do you know how far it is to Harkha? That would take us all night. I can't drive you all the way there."

I reached out to touch him. It would be so easy. But I stopped.

"Please," I said. "Please believe me. I'm absolutely safe, I just need to get to my sisters.

Please don't hand me into the police. You can drop me at the bus station. I promise, I'll be fine."

He looked at me for a while, I could see him weighing up his decision. Finally, he nodded.

"Alright," he said. "I'll drop you at the bus station. But you have to stay there. It's a small town, so I don't know if there will be any buses running overnight, you've probably already missed the last one. And I'll give you some credits for food." He nodded again. "Ok."

I looked at him with curiosity. I'd changed his mind. I'd changed his mind without forcing him, simply by using words. I looked down at my hands in my lap. Perhaps I wasn't that powerful after all. Anyone could do it.

It wasn't long before we pulled up to the bright lights of the bus station.

"Thank you so much for the lift," I said.

"Here. Get yourself something warm to eat. It will probably be a long night." He held out a cyber card. He sighed. "I don't feel right about this."

"You don't need to give me anything."

"I absolutely insist. I won't leave you unless you take it."

I smiled and, as I took the card from him, my finger caught against his. He was wavering, unsure. He'd been flirting with a woman he worked with, and he was struggling to fight the temptation of her. It was flattering, he hadn't thought of himself as being attractive to anyone in a long time. He loved his wife, but he missed the excitement of something new and unfamiliar. Just one night. Surely one night couldn't be too bad. If she never found out.

I pushed a thought into his head. "Thank you," I said.

He wouldn't even notice that woman again. It was only a little nudge. He already loved his wife, and now he'd never want anyone but her.

"I promise that, if I feel unsafe at all, I'll go to the police station." I peered out of the window. "I can see it just there. If I feel at all worried, I'll go."

He nodded. "Stay safe."

I climbed out of the car and slipped the cyber card into my pocket. "Thank you again."

He smiled, and the door slid shut between us. The car hummed, and pulled away. And I was alone.

The bus station was cold and unwelcoming, lit up in sharp fluorescent light, and the rows of metal seating didn't look like an appealing place to spend the whole night. I pushed my hands into my pocket and wrapped my fingers around the cyber card.

I looked around. The pink neon glow of a diner lit the puddles across the street. Hot food. I hadn't thought about eating, but now that I did, my stomach growled ferociously.

The diner was warm, and filled with smells that made my stomach ache. Music played, and the waitress gently sung along as she wiped tables. She was pretty in an effortless kind of way, her long, thick hair drawn back into a pony tail, revealing a line of four moles running up her jaw. She turned to me with tired eyes at odds with the bright smile below them.

"Hello, love," she said.

"Hello," I replied quietly.

The waitress looked expectantly at the door behind me. "All alone?"

"My parents are just at the bus station sorting out tickets for the morning. They sent me over to get something to eat. They'll be here in a little bit."

The waitress nodded and skipped behind the counter. "What can I get for you then? Something nice and hot? You're wet through."

"Yes please, I'm starving." I pulled the cyber card from my pocket and clattered it onto the counter. "My parents gave me this, but I don't know how much is on it."

"No problem, I'll check." She turned her scanner around to face her and flashed the cyber card across it. Her eyes widened as she did. "You better keep this safe, dear." She slid it back to me. "This is way more than one hot meal." She lowered her voice. "This is almost a month's wages."

I stared at the cyber card, scared to pick it up.

"Are you sure your parents are on their way over?"

I looked up at the waitress and attempted a confident, carefree smile. It must have come out a little wrong, however.

"I'll just call someone," she said. "We'll get this sorted."

I launched myself over the counter and grabbed her wrist. She blinked as I pushed the thought into her head. It was more difficult than with the boy, her head was fuller, more jumbled, reluctant. I slid back onto the stool and attempted that carefree smile again.

She looked at me. "Sorry, love, what were you saying?"

"I'll have the full works please." I pointed to a picture on the lit menu screens above her head.

"You must be hungry, that's a big meal for a small tummy."

"I'm starving."

48

OMORI

I was numb when the call ended. I wandered, dizzy and cold to the core, into the living room where Tian was sitting, in his usual place, watching the ocean from the window.

"I need to speak to the whole colony about something," I said. My voice was tiny against the enormity of what I needed to say.

He turned to me, his face full of expectation. It was a look I'd become so familiar with. He was always waiting for what you had to say, always hoping it was the news he longed to hear. When it wasn't, the hope still returned, flaring up again almost instantly. I hated that I had to crush him with more heartbreak, heartbreak he might not recover from quite so easily.

"I want to tell you first, Tian, away from everyone else." I shook my head. How could I even begin to tell him this? I took a deep, shaking breath. "There's been an incident at the Honporo colony. A couple of hours ago, the authorities marched in there. They were taken by complete surprise. They ordered everyone out of their houses, and lined them up. They accused them of terrorism, and gave them no chance to protest the charge. And then they started shooting. Completely at random. I'm so sorry, Tian. Your grandfather has been confirmed as one of the dead."

For a moment, his face didn't change. That hopeful expression hung there, grotesque in the light of what I'd told him. A mask, a habit, as his brain processed what had happened. And then it crumpled. It fell away in flakes. And what was left was raw, and painful, and would leave him scarred. He grabbed the edge of the seat, breathing hard. His shoulders slumped forward, and his chin fell to his chest. And then he toppled towards the floor. I caught him halfway, and eased him down gently.

"I'm so sorry," I whispered, but it would go no way to mending the hurt.

"They looked after me," he whimpered. "They looked after me."

"I know. I need to tell Narata. Everyone needs to know what's happened."

Tian nodded and peeled himself away from me. "I want to come too," he said. "I've heard people here saying things about Honporo, calling them traitors. I've always held my tongue, but I want to be there. I want them to look at me and know that those traders were people, that they were loved."

I nodded. I knew there was no point in trying to dissuade him. Besides, I didn't want to leave him alone, and I wasn't going to break the news to Narata over the phone. There were some things that needed to be said face to face.

I tried to pick Tian up to standing, but he ended up helping me.

"What are we going to do about it?" Tian asked, his face hardening.

"What can we do?"

"I don't know. But there is no way I'm just going to let it go. And I won't let anyone else do that either. I will not let the world forget the Honporo massacre."

"You'll be going up against the government, Tian. Against a public that hate traders now more than ever. I don't think there's anything we can do."

He looked at me with a fire in his eyes that I had never seen before.

"I will not let people forget what happened, and I won't let the government simply turn away from what they've done. Minds can be changed, opinions swayed, and the truth can come to the fore. We need to fight the lies, expose the government for what they're doing to our people."

Pride swelled up inside of me. It caught me by surprise; it came from a pool I didn't even know was there. Pride in Tian, and also pride in traders. Because they were my people too. All of a sudden I felt like an integral part of all this, and for the first time, I felt like I was home. Like I was exactly where I was meant to be. I could see, now, why Kioto had wanted this so badly.

I grabbed Tian's shoulder to steady myself, and I wept. I wept for the lives lost at Honporo, and for the life I'd had taken from me, and I wept for the past, and I wept for the future.

"You're right," I gasped between sobs. "We have to make them listen. We have to show them what they've done."

49

OMORI

Tian was the first one to stand up. That's what we came to call it; the 'standing up'. He had marched into the centre of Okaporo and climbed onto a bench. He had proceeded to read out the names of every trader killed at Honporo. I watched him with pride swelling in my chest.

"Matsu of Honporo. Daughter, sister, mother. Enjoyed old science fiction movies. Killed for terrorism charges. No trial. Nagano of Honporo. Brother, son, uncle. Could drink anyone under the table. Killed for terrorism charges. No trial. Saka of Honporo. Father, brother, son. Unbeaten at chess. Killed for terrorism charges. No trial."

He didn't falter. Not when people stared, or shouted abuse. Not when the first piece of rubbish was thrown at him. And when someone pulled him from his perch, he simply got back up and continued. And he added another name to the list.

"Kioto of Okaporo. Daughter, sister, aunt. Loves the ocean. Imprisoned for terrorism charges. No trial."

On the first day, I had insisted that some of the men from the colony accompanied him. They had stood around him, forming a barricade. On the second day, more traders came. On the third, several took up posts elsewhere in the city and spoke the same words. By day four, they were doing the same in Iwoyo. Honporo followed, and Miyakata, Nagamoto, until every city was filled with the clamour of trader voices.

Tian had said that people just saw traders as a thing, as a whole, as three scars over their right eye. What they needed was to view them as humans, as individuals, as people just like them. It was easy to hate, to turn away when it was just a thing being killed, but when it was people they could relate to, people they had things in common with, they had to listen. They had to care.

He'd been right. Within a week, citizens were standing up too. They formed rings around the traders, held hands with traders, shared their sorrow. Shared their anger. Tian had changed their minds.

"I should be there," I said to Narata. "I should be standing up too."

"You can stand up by sitting right there." She pointed at my sofa. "Sit."

I sat down with a groan. "I should be there," I muttered.

"Jodo is there in your place. And Tian has more support than he could have ever imagined."

"I hate not being a part of this."

Narata rubbed my shoulder. "We're all a part of this. Whether we're stood in the cities, or whether we're keeping the home fires burning, so to speak. And you have the most important job of all, you're creating the first new generation of Okaporo for many, many years. And he needs his mummy to be well rested. So rest. I will tie you down if I have to."

I eyed her suspiciously. "You wouldn't."

"Jodo gave me his permission." She grinned. "And imagine what he'd do to me if I let you go marching around Okaporo in your condition. That man could snap me like a twig."

I laughed. "He could. But he wouldn't. My gentle giant." I sighed and looked down at the floor.

"Don't do that. Don't feel guilty for living your life. Kioto wouldn't have wanted you to put everything on hold."

"I know. But... I just..."

"It's not easy to let yourself be happy while she's still locked up, I know that. But look what you've done. When she gets released, she'll have a home to come to, and a sister, a brother-in-law, a beautiful nephew. Not so long ago she thought she had no family left at all. But you've given her one. It's not like you've skipped off and fallen in love and forgotten all about her."

I nodded. "I just wish she was here now."

"Look at what Tian's done. There are citizens protesting for her release. When did we ever think we'd see that?"

"Do you think the government will bow to the pressure."

"If we push hard enough."

"Everything just seems to take so long. Dai's always complaining about it. It's all talk and talk and talk." I patted my stomach. "Goodness knows how old this one will be before he gets to meet his Auntie Kioto."

I jumped as the front door flew open. Firefinch bundled into the room, closely followed by Malia.

"Dai's on TV," Firefinch gasped.

He stretched out the small screen he had between his hands, and threw it against the far wall. We all stared at it.

Dai was fidgeting in the suit they'd obviously insisted he wore. His hair was combed, his complexion smoothed with cosmetics. My mouth fell open. He was barely recognisable.

"He always swore he'd never do this," Narata said, shaking her head.

"Well," said Firefinch, "if they made him do it, they're going to be sorry they did. I think he may have gone off script somewhat."

"I'm not the hero," Dai was saying. "I never have been, and I don't want to be seen as one. I don't deserve any kind of adoration. I'm a poster boy." He laughed and gestured towards his face. "If you can believe that."

"I don't know," laughed the host. "I can see it.

In a rugged, man-of-the-wilds kind of a way."

"The government needed a face, and mine was the one that fitted. The true hero has been betrayed, completely and utterly. And by me, too. I should have done more. I should have refused to play along."

"Who is the real hero?" the host asked.

Dai looked directly at the camera. "Kioto of Okaporo."

"The name they're shouting in the streets."

"Absolutely."

"Tell us about Kioto."

"She single-handedly wiped out every single Qathab vessel."

"The people who can put thoughts into other people's heads. Make them do whatever they want them to do."

"Right. They were putting compulsions into people's heads to kill government officials. They didn't even shed the blood with their own hands. And Kioto killed them all. It was her plan. And she put her own sister in mortal danger by doing it. She did it to save Lobaya."

"But she didn't get a hero's parade, did she?"

"Not at all. The government didn't want a trader to be the hero of the story."

"Not a good look."

Dai shook his head. "No. So she got to be the scapegoat instead. For almost two years she's been locked up in a high security prison without trial, without visitation rights, without any contact with the outside world at all. And for what? Charges constructed out of thin air that she has never been convicted of. No trial at all. No hope of one either. How is that fair?"

"It doesn't seem fair to me."

"Kioto is the real hero. And she needs to be released immediately. With a full pardon." He turned back to the camera again. "We need you to march in the streets, to take your voices to the government buildings, and don't stop shouting until Kioto is free."

50

NOLA

I sat up and blinked. Through the small window above me I could see the sky beginning to lighten, deep blue giving way to gold. I stretched out my aching joints and looked around.

I had spent the night in a small back room of the diner. It was nothing special; just a couple of old armchairs, a small table, and a stack of cardboard boxes.

The diner was already waking up, with the morning rush stumbling in for coffee and bagels. I slipped into a booth as if I'd just come in, and the waitress hurried over.

"On your own, love?" I looked up at her and smiled. Dark rings hung under her eyes. She'd slept in the other armchair, not that she would remember that.

"No, my parents are just sorting out bus tickets, they sent me over here to have some breakfast."

"What can I get you then, sweetheart?" she asked, as if she'd never met me before. But then, as far as she could remember, she hadn't.

"Pancakes."

"Ice cream?"

I nodded.

"Syrup?"

I nodded again.

"Anything to drink?"

"Milkshake, please."

She eyed me closely. "I bet banana's your favourite. Am I right?"

"You are."

She nodded. "Work here long enough and you learn. You look like a banana milkshake kind of girl." She bent down and whispered "It's my favourite too."

I brushed her hand. After work today she'd finally leave her cheating boyfriend. She didn't love him, she just needed the confidence to go through with it. She had it now, and she deserved so much better.

With my stomach full, I paid, leaving a very generous tip, and set off towards the bus station.

The bus ran for two hours straight before stopping. When it did, everyone tumbled off and took deep breaths, stretching out their cramped limbs, and filling their bodies with the freshness of the world.

I pulled out the crumpled map I'd picked up at the bus station. We were on the outskirts of Qatkha and the land here was flat and featureless. I could see the city in the distance, like a smudge across the desert.

On my tourist map, Qatkha was surrounded by pictures of rolls of fabrics, and weaving machines. I wondered how much of its traditional industry still remained. People had probably been replaced by machines, like they had everywhere, churning out reams and reams every hour, never stopping for a break, working all day and all night. And finishing off with a quaint little label, suggesting that it was traditionally made, authentic, when it was nothing of the sort. Everything was pretending to be something it wasn't.

I looked over at the squat building we'd stopped at. It was a convenience store, with a small coffee shop attached to the side. At the other end were the toilets, and I made my way over to them.

The toilet block was exactly what I'd expected; designed to protect itself against any expense caused by relentless vandalism and graffiti. The toilets were stainless steel, the seats fixed in place, and the basins were set into recesses in the walls. There were no mirrors, no niceties, nothing that wasn't designed merely for function. It was a box, with no windows, and a heavy door that swung shut behind me. I could imagine women being scared in here.

I heard the door open, and the footfall sounded too heavy to be female. The boots that stopped outside my cubicle were heavy work boots. And they were big.

I re-dressed quietly and stared at the cubicle door, picturing the person on the other side. I slid back the lock, and pulled the door open quickly. The man was humongous. I barely even reached his navel. I ducked past him and crossed to the basin.

"Aren't you young to be travelling alone?" he asked.

I shrugged. "I'm ok."

"Maybe I could look after you. Keep you safe, like."

I turned around. "No, thank you." As I moved to leave, he stepped into my path.

"There's a lot of bad people out there that would look to take advantage of a sweet little thing like you." He licked his thick lips.

"I'm not that sweet."

"You look sweet to me. Juicy and sweet. Like a little peach."

I tried to duck past him, and he moved again to block me.

"Maybe I'll just take a small bite." He bent down close and gnashed his teeth.

Instinctively, I reached out to grab his hand, but found only thick leather gloves. I saw the flash of a blade, and panic turned everything upside down. Everyone at the centre had been wrong; I did have something to be scared of. I still bled like other people, and I would still die like them.

I scrabbled and fought, but I was a mouse

struggling in the grip of a bear. I needed to find skin. He found it first, the blade stinging and burning as it sliced into my flesh. I scrambled up his hulk, my hands finding thick clothes; wool, leather, tweed, denim, waxed cotton. And then, finally, the softness of his neck.

I dropped from him, slipping in a slick of blood, and stumbled towards the door. I looked back. He drove the knife into himself over and over, as he sank towards the floor. The knife fell from his grip, and he took his last, shallow breath.

As I reclaimed my seat on the bus, nauseated, I stared at my hollow reflection in the window. My stomach was a rock, hard and unforgetting, and my eyes were dry with the grittiness of regret.

The bus went no further than Harkha. Nothing did anymore. After Lobaya declared war on Qathab, Merhan allied with Lobaya, and the borders were closed. But that wasn't a big issue for me. All it meant was that I had a bit of a walk.

The border guards took instructions easily; they were used to it, designed for obedience, and the thought to let me cross the border slipped into their minds as if they'd decided it for themselves.

Merhan was very different to Qathab. Despite the Qathab mountains being contained in the north of the country, their presence was felt all the way down to the flats of Harkha, with rocky outcrops bursting out of the ground. It was as if the mountains were rooted like trees, their stone tendrils stretched out under the whole country.

Merhan, however, was green. Known as 'The Garden of the World', its meadows rippled across the land, the peacock grass wavering and glinting in the breeze as if it were an ocean, and I, a tiny boat. The air was filled with the sweet scent of flowers, the dusky aroma of trees, and the tang of wild garlic. I turned my head towards the breeze and caught the smell of hay drying in the fields, and the reek of cattle.

I turned my head towards Lobaya. Towards the sea. That's what called me, deep inside. In some ancient part of me.

Maraai was Merhan's capital, a city pushed up against the border with Lobaya. It was busy, international, and filled with exotic accents and languages.

As I looked up at the Central Bus Station I couldn't repress the sharp intake of breath. Nor could the other people whose stride faltered as they approached, whose eyes squinted from the glare, but couldn't draw themselves away from the structure entirely. Made purely of glass, radiant in the sunlight, its roof swept over the top in a series of elegant curves. Several panes of glass were coloured, here and there, as if a rainbow had fallen from the sky and shattered on landing. The approach was a straight avenue of trees that had been trimmed of all their lower branches, giving them a tall, slender look. Their bark was a pale grey, covered in a short, velvet-like fur. Among their branches hung small fruits, deep purple and aromatic.

I pushed my way through the crowd inside and looked up at the departure screens. Buses came in and out of Maraai every few minutes, constantly changing its population, like sand moved by the tide. I looked for buses to Ayyil, so that I could cross into Lobaya via the hills of Kumonayo. Unexpected. Undetected. Lobaya was not about to welcome another vessel from Qathab.

And then I would keep going until I hit the coast at Okaporo.

51

KIOTO

The interview rooms were located below the prison, in the basement, accessed via a set of concrete steps. They were obviously old cells; tiny, cramped spaces, with thick, metal doors. There were no windows down here, no hint of there even being a world outside. And it was cold, and damp, in a way that ate into your bones and left you shivering for hours after.

In the two years I'd been here, they'd marched me down to the interview rooms just a handful of times, all of them within the last two months. I didn't have a lawyer to come and see me, and they didn't allow me any visitors. Sometimes they told me that my friends didn't want to come, but I knew it wasn't true. They could lock me up forever if they wanted, but they could never turn me against the people I loved.

My body slumped when I saw the suit waiting for me. Despite telling myself over and over not to hope that it would be Dai again, part of me had, and that part was now left disappointed.

The man turned and looked at me as I was brought over. He wasn't a lawyer; he appeared to be more nervous than I was. I'd come to recognise the look that settled into the eyes of everyone who frequented this place. A look that had given up hope of there being any good left in the world. His eyes still had hope.

He stood up as I entered the room, and offered his hand for shaking.

"Who are you?" I asked, ignoring his gesture.

"I am your PR manager," he said. "I'm Kinawa Honoka."

"You're my what?"

"PR. It stands for public relations—"

"I know what it means," I snapped. "I'm just wondering why, exactly, I would need you."

"I have some contracts for you to sign." He fumbled through the stack of papers on the desk.

"Contracts for what?"

"Erm... Your compliance."

I held up my hands. "Stop. You're just confusing me more and more every time you open your mouth. Start from the beginning."

He took a deep breath. "Your release—"

"My what?"

"Your release."

I looked up at the guard who had escorted me down. He shrugged.

"I'm getting released?"

"I was led to believe that you had already been informed. I'm sorry. I didn't mean to break the news so..." He shook his head. "I thought you knew."

"Is this real?"

He nodded, half a smile cautiously lighting his face.

"They're releasing me?"

"On some conditions."

I wrapped my arms tightly around myself as the room started to spin. I stumbled to the chair opposite Kinawa and slumped into it. I wanted to scream, cry, slam my hands against the walls. I looked back up at Kinawa. "When?"

"I don't know. These things take time, I will warn you of that. There are a lot of documents that need to be rubber stamped, and the government certainly like their rubber stamps. It could be a while yet, so don't get too excited."

"Too excited? There is finally, finally an end to this. An ending where, before, there was just eternity. Say what you like, I'll be swinging from the ceiling until I'm out of here."

"Well, I've warned you, it might take a while."

"I don't care. I'm getting out."

"Like I said, there are conditions."

"Whatever, yes, whatever."

"Your release is completely dependent on your cooperation in all PR matters. You will say what you are told to say, do what you are told to do, wear what you are told to wear. You'll go where you're told, stand how you're told, and you won't even breathe unless it's been pre-approved. Do you understand?"

I nodded, but his words were merely rushing past me. I could be agreeing to anything, but it didn't matter. All I could see was Omori's face, and I could feel my nephew nestled in my arms, and Tian. I could see Tian. And we would watch the ocean together as it breathed in and out against the shore.

"You will, basically, be the government's PR puppet. And I will not leave your side. You will do every tiny thing I tell you to, even if it seems ridiculous, even if it goes against everything you believe. Do you understand?"

"Yes, yes," I said, with a wave of my hand.

He pushed some papers towards me. "Would you like to have time to think about it?"

"No, where do I sign?"

"You really should read it first."

"I'm sure it's fine."

He placed his hand over the contract. "I strongly suggest you take it away, read it carefully, and think hard about what you want to do."

"Ok, I'll read it."

"Once you sign this, the government own you. And if you so much as sneeze in a way they don't like, you'll be back in here and you will never see daylight again."

52

OMORI

I padded back into the living room, still groggy after a long nap. I poured myself a drink and looked through the cupboards for something to eat. They were stacked with food; full of all the things I'd insisted Jodo had to go out and buy me straight away, to satisfy some new craving, things that, as soon as he'd presented it to me, usually with a look of triumph on his face, I no longer wanted. And I didn't want any of it now, either.

"Why is there never anything to eat around here?" I said out loud.

Today there was no one to reply. No one to indulge my pregnant ravings. I peered into the empty living room. Tian was in Okaporo, still reading out names. I missed him.

Wandering over to the window seat, I settled myself into the Tian-shaped indentation in the cushion, and gazed out of the window.

The sun shone brightly today, and the water glistened as if strings of diamonds had fallen from a passing ship. Gulls wheeled and dipped in the cloudless sky, above colourful fishing boats heading back to the harbour. It was perfect. If I could have sent a photo to Kioto, I would have.

It hadn't taken long for me to connect with the sea. I obviously still had salt water in my veins, even though I'd never known it. I loved this place, and they'd have to tear me away from it if they ever wanted me to leave.

"And you'll love it too," I whispered to my stomach. The baby shifted, rolling over inside of me, as if in agreement. "And you'll love your Auntie Kioto. And she's going to love you so much." My eyes ached with tears, and I blinked them away.

As I leant back against the cool window glass, I could hear the mumble of voices outside. I scrambled onto my knees and peered out. Jodo was talking to someone. He had his back to me, and his hulk masked whoever he was speaking with, but I saw their hands as they gesticulated, shooting out from either side of Jodo as if he had an extra set.

I leaned further forward, trying to find a better angle, and bumped my head against the window.

Jodo turned. He didn't smile. His face was a sheet of worry, which I would have been able to read even if he'd tried to mask it with a smile. I loved that he knew me well enough not to even try.

I climbed down from my perch and pulled the front door open, buffeted in the face by a strong wind. It wouldn't stop me from finding out what was going on. I marched out, head down.

"Dai," I said. "What are you doing here?"

"Let's all go inside and sit down, shall we?" said Jodo.

"What's going on?" I demanded. Jodo pushed me back towards the house. "Is it Kioto? Has something happened to her?" I spun around and pounded uselessly on Jodo's chest. "You tell me right now!"

Dai rolled his eyes. "She's getting more like her sister, isn't she?"

"Only since she got pregnant," Jodo replied.

"Do not talk about me like I don't exist." I could hear my voice becoming shrill, but I couldn't steady it. "Tell me what's happened. Now."

Dai placed his hand on my shoulder. He glanced up at Jodo. "It is about Kioto. But it's not bad news. The government have signed the papers for her release."

I instantly realised why Jodo had looked so worried, and he'd been right to. My legs buckled, but his hands were ready to catch me. He scooped me up into his arms and carried me inside.

"You've got to understand," said Dai, "that nothing this government does ever happens quickly. There will be paperwork. So much paperwork. It will have to go through about twenty different departments. It will sit in to-do piles for weeks on end. This will not happen quickly. It could be months before you have her home."

"But I will have her home," I whispered. "I want to be the one to tell Tian."

Dai nodded. "Of course."

"And you'll keep me up to date with everything. I want to know every tiny detail. I want to know whose desk her papers are on when." I knew that I was gabbling, and making unreasonable demands, but my heart was beating so fast that it felt like I was tumbling over and over.

"I doubt I'll be privy to any of that. But every time I find something out, I promise I'll call you. The other thing is that her release comes with conditions. They've made up a PR contract that says she has to do whatever the government tell her, or she's back inside. And you know what Kioto's like. Now, I haven't seen the contract myself, but I was told that it holds no end date. She's under contract to the government until they decide to release her from it. So, she's not completely free. She might never be."

"What are they going to make her say?"

"It will be carefully scripted press reports, interviews, publicity campaigns. They might have her all over the country. You might hardly see her. She'll be at their beck and call. Forever, if they want to."

I nodded. "But surely they will let her come home."

"I'm sure they will. I just don't know when. The call for her release was so public, that they're going to want to make a big ceremony out of it. The government listening to its people. They're going to really play on that. It's going to be huge. And it will probably keep her wrapped up in all kinds of PR dances for several months. It could be a long time before they give her leave to come back."

"On the other hand," said Jodo, "might they want to do a big thing about her coming back here? What with Okaporo's history, it would be an emotive spin on things."

"That's right, they could," said Dai. "But don't count on it. Just understand that your family reunion is in the hands of the government. A government that has had that hand forced."

"I understand."

Jodo took my shaking hands in his. "And you need to stay calm. For little one's sake. You only have a few weeks left, but he's still got a lot of growing to do. He needs his mummy calm and rested."

If only Jodo could have seen the somersaults my stomach was doing, seen my heart swelling, ready to burst, seen every single part of me tingling. I'd keep it under wraps, but nothing would stop me looking forward to having Kioto back. And every part of me filled with a hope she'd be home in time to see the birth of her nephew.

53

KIOTO

I shook my head. "No way. No deal."

"You've already signed the contract," said Kinawa.

I looked at him, at his crisp suit, at his twitching fingers. He was probably aching to open a screen, to connect to the world, to do whatever it was people did on those things all day. The prison had a blocker installed, his implants were useless.

"I know I've already signed it, but I'm not moving on this. Keep me locked up if you want."

Kinawa sighed and dragged his fingers back through his slick hair. "It would make for amazing TV. The emotional reunion between the triumphant hero, Kioto, and her poor, desperate sister."

"Heavily pregnant sister."

He pointed a chewed pen at me. "Exactly. People will love it. Just about to pop, and she still travelled across the country to be the first one to see you freed."

"Move on, Kinawa, it's not happening. She's due in just two weeks. There is no way I'm making her travel all the way here just for the sake of ratings."

He sighed again. "My bosses won't be happy."

I tapped the desk between us. "How about this, we have an emotional reunion between myself and Dai here at the prison. The 'triumphant hero, Kioto' and her mortal enemy who, through the most trying of times, became a firm friend and ally." I fanned my hands out dramatically.

Kinawa resumed the chewing of his pen. He hummed thoughtfully. Then he nodded. "That could work. I'll pitch it." He made a note on his pad.

"Then," I continued, "we go straight to Okaporo, Kioto's long-lost home, the scene of the massacre that, as far as young Kioto knew, killed her entire family, a home that was almost lost to her again when the government concreted over it—"

"But," interjected Kinawa, "that the government returned to the traders of Okaporo in a gesture of selfless good will. A hand offered forward in peace."

I rolled my eyes. "Yeah, whatever. So, we do the emotional reunion between sisters there, on the streets of Okaporo, because Omori, despite desperately wanting to have met Kioto at the gates of the prison, was unable to travel so far because of her condition."

Kinawa nodded thoughtfully. "That could definitely work. The homecoming. Compelling stuff."

"So that's settled?"

Kinawa leaned back in his chair and awkwardly laced his hands behind his head. I appreciated his efforts, but it was clear that being in the prison still spooked him.

"I'll talk my bosses round. Put a good spin on it."

"I'm sure you're very good at putting spins on things," I replied.

He gave me a lopsided smile. "It's what I'm paid to do."

"So, when is this happening? When am I actually getting out of here?"

"Soon. Very soon. Just a few more contracts to be signed on that all-important dotted line, and we're good to go."

It didn't really matter, in my mind I was already there. Stood on the warm sand, the sea licking my toes. Gulls screaming above me, bells ringing with the sway of the boats. Salt on my lips. In the five years since I'd found Omori, I'd done hardly any extractions, and I hadn't needed to hold the memories myself. In that time, my own memories had strengthened, stretching themselves out in my head, filling the space that was often so cluttered with other people's thoughts. And two years locked away had given me too much time to ponder them, and for them to refine themselves, to focus, and increase their vibrancy. When you removed the clamour and distractions of life, your memories had the opportunity to come to the fore. I had been living in a powerful recreation of Okaporo for some time. So real that I could sometimes touch it.

"As soon as I know, you'll know," Kinawa was saying.

I blinked, returning to the room. "Right. Thank you."

He nodded and stood up. "Stay positive."

I smiled, the winds of Okaporo moving through my hair.

54

OMORI

I jumped as Tian's hand fell onto my arm.

"What were you thinking about?" he asked.

"Sorry, yeah, miles away."

"It won't be long now. She'll be home soon."

"Is it really bad that I'm a bit nervous about it?"

Tian smiled and shook his head slightly. "Is it bad that I am too?"

"It's just that we've all made a life here, and everything's so different to how it was two years ago. I'm different. I'm a wife now, almost a mother, and I feel so responsible for this place." I laughed. "This place that I once insisted meant nothing to me."

"It really meant nothing to me once upon a time," Tian said.

"And now?"

"I couldn't imagine being anywhere else."

I squeezed his arm. "We wouldn't want you to be. You're like a brother to me now." I sighed. "I mean, I think it's ok for me to feel worried about how Kioto's going to feel coming here. It's not quite the Okaporo she envisioned returning to. It's more like a town than a colony. We even have shops and restaurants."

"A night club," said Tian.

"Right. And we have rogues living alongside traders. I mean, is that really the vision she had for this place? But it's ok, it's ok for me to worry about how she's going to feel. But—" I instinctively dropped my voice to a whisper. "It's really, really awful that part of me is worried that she's going to spoil it. I love what we have here. I love the mix of modern and traditional. To be honest, I really don't want to live in a makeshift shack. What if she ruins everything we have here?" I shook my head. "It's really bad that I'm thinking that, isn't it?"

Tian shrugged. "Everything's about to change, and we have no idea what things will look like afterwards. It's ok to be scared about that. It's normal. I'm scared that she won't want me around anymore. I'm not a proper trader, after all."

"You are a proper trader. And no one here would ever say different."

"Maybe not out loud."

I looked at him and laughed brightly. "Listen to us. All these doubts about who we are and where we belong in Kioto's life. We're going to be back in it, and that's all that..." I drifted off, leaving the sentence unfinished. I stared out at the sea.

"Omori? Are you ok?" Tian ventured.

I shot my hand up to silence him.

"What is it?"

I frowned and shook my head. "It can't be."

"What?"

"Tian. A vessel has just crossed into Lobaya."

"That's impossible, Omori. Are you sure?"

"Absolutely certain."

55

KIOTO

I looked down at the outfit they'd dressed me in. I would have preferred the prison uniform. It was a long dress, sheer layers of floral fabrics in gentle hues, interspersed with layers of white lace. A long, sleeveless cardigan completed the look, and I was surprised it wasn't hemmed with fringing or adorned with bells. It screamed stereotype. They'd also, unsurprisingly, pulled my hair back from my face, plaiting the sides so that I had no opportunity to hide my trader scars. It was pitifully obvious. Overly so. Like I was playing dress-up.

"Would you like me to skip out playing a tambourine?" I asked Kinawa sourly.

"Play nice," he said. "I think you look great."

"You would," I snarled.

"Dai will be waiting for you outside. If you could muster up some tears, that would be perfect. Try not to look directly at the cameras, but be aware of them. They want to see your face, so try not to turn your back on them. Is that ok?"

"Maybe I could perform a jig?"

"Just follow the script. You're getting released, Kioto, after two years of unfair imprisonment. Can you at least manage a smile?"

"I don't smile."

"You do now. We have a contract that says you will."

I flashed him a broad smile.

"That's better. Come on, your public awaits."

I sighed and stood up. As I did, my hands clenched into fists. I tried to move, but my legs were as stiff as the walls, my feet stuck to the floor. I looked at Kinawa desperately, my heart beating fast.

"It's just hit you, hasn't it?"

I nodded once, quickly. I couldn't speak, couldn't cover my fear with more sarcasm.

He reached out and took hold of my hand. "I'll be right beside you, and Dai's waiting just beyond the gates. I've already spoken to him this morning, and he's so excited."

"I can't do it," I whispered. I'd never felt so small, so helpless. So see-through.

"You can. Think of that little nephew of yours. He's going to be coming into the world really soon, and he'll want to see his auntie. His strong, independent, brave auntie. You're not going to deny him that, are you?"

I looked down at his hand in mine. "You have surprisingly dainty hands. They're just like a little girl's."

"There you go, that's the sarcastic, mean Kioto I know. Come on, let's get out of this shithole."

I tossed my head and held my chin high. I didn't feel brave—I was a wreck inside—but I was sure as anything that I would walk out looking like the bravest woman in the world. Even if I was in a ridiculous costume.

I would ignore all of Kinawa's instructions; I wasn't going to come out blinking like I hadn't seen sunlight in two years. And I certainly wasn't going to run to Dai and jump into his arms. If anything, I was going to punch him in the face for not getting me out sooner.

But as the gates closed behind me, and I saw Dai waiting, with a cyclorama of cameras behind him, the mask slipped from my face. I did run to him, I did throw myself into his arms, and I cried and cried and cried. Not for the cameras, not for Kinawa, but because my heart wouldn't let me do anything else.

He held me so tightly, and for such a long time. When we finally parted, his cheeks were wet.

"Are you crying?" I said.

"Watch out, Kioto, you almost showed some emotion then."

I made a show of glancing around. "It's ok, I think I managed to cover it with some sarcasm."

Dai laughed. "Almost. Almost. How does it feel

to be free?"

"I'd like to be free of these stupid clothes."

He looked me up and down. "Yeah... I can see why." He laughed again. "Everyone in Okaporo is desperate to see you."

"Omori hasn't had her baby yet, has she? I was really hoping..."

"Don't worry, you're still in time to see your nephew born. The first baby born in Okaporo for years."

"You know what's fitting? Omori was actually the last baby born in Okaporo, before..."

"Really? That's amazing. She'll love that."

"I'm surprised Narata hasn't pointed it out already." I shrugged. "Maybe she'd forgotten."

Dai patted my shoulder. "Maybe. We should get going, and I bet you're keen to get home."

"You have no idea."

"But there's something I need to tell you first. Omori called me earlier. She says that a vessel has just crossed the border."

I shook my head. "That's impossible. We killed them all."

"You killed them all," he corrected. "But apparently not all of them."

"What do we do?"

"I've had to inform the authorities. Kioto, they want to turn it into a PR stunt."

"What? They're crazy."

"They want you to prove yourself. They want you to kill the vessel. On live TV."

56

NÔLA

The green hills of Merhan had flowed seamlessly into the hills of Lobaya; I hadn't even realised I'd crossed the border until I'd seen Kumonayo in the distance.

As I approached the centre of the city, the squat houses giving way to huge, glass-encased tower blocks, I saw posters and banners featuring Kioto's name, sometimes her face, sometimes just the image of an eye crossed with three scars. But, equally, there were posters demonising her, and all traders. Violent, hateful words scrawled onto the sides of buildings. Lobaya was divided, and Kioto stood in that divide.

My hand raised to my own face, and I felt a wave of regret. What if they rejected me? I was the enemy, I knew that. What if they took my self-inflicted scars to be a mockery, an insult? As if I were a child who had drawn them on with pen. Whatever I felt inside, this was not my culture, I hadn't grown up as a part of it.

I reached up and tugged my hair lose, letting the curls fall over my face.

I had already felt Omori's presence, and I was certain that she'd already be aware of me. There was too much distance between us for a full connection, but once I was closer to Okaporo, we'd be able to talk. I could explain. I only hoped that she would listen. I didn't want to carry the sins of my people, I wanted to wear the scars of my sisters.

I found my way to the colony easily enough; a line of streamers led me there. The gateway was filled with candles, their flickering flames lighting pictures of Kioto. People had left cyber cards, tokens, scraps of material were tied around the railings, and helium balloons bobbed above them. A small crowd of visitors were gathered there, mostly taking selfies and recording videos, chatting away to their online followers. Their jackets were adorned with button badges. I couldn't read the text from where I stood, but I could see Kioto's face on some, a scarred eye logo on another. I smiled. Everyone had their own religion, and they'd adopted Kioto as their deity.

"Kioto's little sister, Omori, lived right here at the Kumonayo colony for a few years," someone was saying to a screen. "Kioto herself has visited here. More exciting than that, Kioto's parents are buried here, and their graves have become a place of pilgrimage. I'll take you there next."

I held my hand against my suddenly cold chest and breathed hard. My father was buried here. Dazed, I turned and walked into the colony. It was busy here too, with people taking photos like it was a tourist attraction. The older traders seemed to be staying out of sight, but the children and teenagers were enjoying the attention, giving interviews and posing for photos, their fingers extended into peace signs.

"This is where Kioto's parents lived with Omori." A young trader was stood in front of one of the houses, giving some kind of talk. "If you'd like to come inside, I can show you around where they lived. Omori's bedroom is just as she left it the day she was torn from her mother's arms, taken as part of the government's ruthless and cruel liberation programme. There is an extra fee to enter the house, simply to preserve the site. It's an important part of Kioto's story, and we need to ensure it's kept safe so that other people can visit."

Several people surged forward, cyber cards held aloft.

I followed the flow of people to the far end of the colony, where there lay a flat, open meadow. The graves of the ancestors were clearly designated with stone markers, scattered with flowers and tokens, but they paled beside the festival on the hillside.

A large bonfire crackled and spat, its flames

clawing their way high into the sky above. Around it, people danced, in various states of undress. Their arms snaked above their heads, as if they themselves burnt as part of the pyre. Drums boomed, echoing across the hills. And the sweet smell of herbal cigarettes accompanied the aurora of orange stars that glowed as they were inhaled.

I'd never even imagined anything like this before. My life had been filled with regiment, and rules, restrictions, and sterility. These people weren't bound by anything, tossing off social norms like they had their clothes. Not constrained by propriety, or deference, or even shame.

I'd spent my life wishing I was someone else, trying to break free from the mould I was being forced into. Part of me wanted to run over, pull off clothes, and dance until I collapsed. But I couldn't shed my training so easily. Qathab was a country of restraint, a country of solemnity. Nothing was done purely out of frivolity. Everything needed purpose, and a measurable outcome, and permission.

I wasn't the only one watching from a safe distance, lacking the abandonment to participate.

"I bet the traders are hating this." I jumped as someone nudged my elbow. "Everyone tramping all over their ancestors." The guy laughed, all gums and teeth, like a horse. "They're funny about that."

I looked at him. "Yeah, right, how odd that they might be upset about that lot dancing all over the graves of people they loved. Or people they would have liked the chance to have loved."

"Yeah. Whatever." He sidled away.

All of this was nothing more than a trend, a fad. No one really believed in it, not deeply, not enough that they'd stay true to it once popular culture became obsessed with something else. Kioto was the people's hero today, but there was no knowing what she might become tomorrow. It was in the hands of the people, and they were truly fickle.

A cheer went up from the people by the bonfire, and it was echoed by others. Screens lit up, people gathered round.

"She's free!" someone cried out.

"Kioto's been released!"

I pushed through a tight group of people and peered at someone's screen. They jabbed with their elbows, pushing the crush back, and pulled the screen bigger. We watched, in awed silence, as Kioto ran from the building into the arms of an awaiting man.

"That's Dai," someone said. "He's a rogue."

"A rogue? That can't be right. She hates them," someone else responded.

Eyes were rolled as voices began to clamour around us.

"Are you serious? She's been running with a bunch of rogues for years now. He's their leader."

"He seems a bit old for her."

"Sugar daddy."

"Child snatcher."

"Well, good on him, I say. I wouldn't say no to her."

"He's the famous vessel killer."

"But she's the one that killed them all. In one

241

go. Like a huge psychic explosion. Pow!"

Emotions erupted inside me, tangled together like a thicket of moods and passions, so that I could no longer unpick them to name them individually. I gasped for breath, my hands clutched into my gut. My head began to spin, the world flipping around me. I felt like I was falling, and then, my mind exploded, and I was a void, a cavern where my tiny self could only stare at the immense empty space around it. My breath escaped me in an efflux that bent me double. I scrabbled for something to grab hold of, but my fingers found only air as people backed away. I dropped, panting and choking, and the cool grass caught me.

57

OMORI

As the pain tore through my skull, my hand went automatically to my stomach, not to my head. My baby lurched, arching his back as the swell coursed through his tiny body.

I sat down heavily, all of my limbs shaking. And then I felt it. It began in the small of my back, radiating out through my stomach. I bent forward and grabbed the edge of the coffee table.

I heard something smash; crockery dropped. And a pair of huge hands gripped my shoulders.

"What is it? Is it the baby?" Jodo asked, his voice tight.

"It's nothing," I shooed him away, but he didn't move.

"Is the baby coming?"

"No, the baby is not coming. It's just one contraction. That happens sometimes. It's nothing."

"Let's get you to the hospital, just in case."

"No," I snapped. And then, "No," more calmly. "Besides, I'm not having him in the hospital, I'm having him here. And Kioto's on her way. I have to be here when she arrives."

"But we don't have a trained midwife here, Omori. And Kioto won't be here for hours yet."

"I've already organised with the midwife from Iwoyo. It's all in hand."

"Then let's call her."

"It's nothing. Everything's fine."

Jodo came around to the front of me. "Either you let me call the midwife, or I will pick you up and carry you to the hospital. And you know that I will."

I did. "Fine, call the midwife."

I carefully eased myself back on the sofa. I shifted from side to side, trying to encourage the baby to move. He didn't.

I could hear Jodo in the kitchen, talking to the midwife. "Come on, little one," I whispered.

Whatever that was that the vessel had sent out, it had been so full of confusion, and anguish, it didn't feel intentional. This vessel wasn't like the others that had come from Qathab.

I rubbed my stomach, pressing hard with my hand, panic coursing through me. I begged him to move, to be alright. I didn't know how I could love someone so fiercely when I hadn't even met them yet. Finally, he pushed back. I lay my pounding head down, and closed my eyes.

58

KIOTO

"This is insane," I whispered to Dai. We were sat in the back of an auto car, speeding towards Okaporo. "I can't kill someone, and on live TV? What are they thinking?"

"They're thinking about one thing. Ratings. I heard them talking earlier. Your release gave them the highest ratings they've ever seen. Ever. They're not going to give that up easily."

I shook my head in disbelief. "I don't even know how to fire a gun."

Dai patted my hand. "It's the Kioto channel now. They own you."

I dropped my head onto the back of the seat. "All I want to do is go home."

"That's where we're headed right now.

Everyone's waiting for you."

"Yeah, along with this little circus."

He nudged me. "It's your circus now."

I stared at my hands screwed tightly together between my knees. "I can't do this," I said.

"You've done it before."

"Not like this. I've never pointed a gun at someone and pulled the trigger. I may have orchestrated the destruction of the vessels, but I didn't do it with my own hands. I didn't have to stand and watch anyone die." I shook my head. "I've never even fired a gun before."

"Just remember that they're the enemy. You're the good guy. Girl. Whatever."

"It doesn't feel like it."

"Look, there's an easy way out of this."

I looked up at him. "Yeah, I relinquish my freedom forever."

"No. Weren't you listening? They said they'd have a hidden sniper, just in case it went wrong. If you didn't manage to kill the vessel, he would. They hardly want it broadcast on live TV if your bullet just shears off part of the face and the vessel's writhing around on the floor in agony. They want a clean kill. Quick. Neat and tidy. All you need to do is miss. The sniper will do the rest. And it's not like you haven't held a gun to someone's head before, is it?"

I looked away as I felt my cheeks flush.

"Blimey," Dai said. "And you enjoyed it, didn't you? That feeling of power. Knowing that you held someone's life in your hands." He nudged me hard.

"You are a ruthless killer after all."

"Shut up, Dai," I muttered.

"We'll make a rogue out of you yet."

I screwed my hands into fists, digging my fingernails into my fleshy palms. But I had enjoyed it. I couldn't deny that. I glanced at Dai. Even in his PR costume he still had a feather pinned to his jacket. A rogue to the bitter end. He'd never change. He was supposed to be everything that I hated, but I was proving to be more like him than I'd ever care to admit. And now this. They were thrusting a gun into my hands for the sake of entertainment. I was supposed to put a bullet into someone, end their life, for ratings. As if a life meant nothing. Although, in truth, this life was the price of my freedom. That's how it was being valued. I would have to live with this forever, and my shoulders were already weighed down with the burdens I carried.

"I can't do it," I said aloud. "I won't. They can lock me up again if they want to. I can't have yet another face that haunts me. I've wronged too many people already."

"Don't be so melodramatic. You've done exactly what everyone else on this planet does every single day: you've made a decision based on the knowledge from your own perspective. And you've preserved your own life, and the lives of people who are important to you. That doesn't make you some kind of movie villain, it makes you human. It's nature. It's how our species has survived. How any species survives. Do you think a lioness is weighing up all the moral arguments when she makes a kill to feed her cubs? Or when she kills to protect them?"

"I'm not a lioness."

"But you are just another animal. We all are." He growled at me, and I sneered in reply. "There, you see?" He laughed.

"What's it like to kill someone?"

Dai took a deep breath, and exhaled it with a sharp sigh. "I know you're looking for something thoughtful and philosophical here, but I'm afraid I'll disappoint you. The truth is, it's different for everyone. For me, it's just business. Like signing a contract."

"How can you be so emotionless?"

Dai rolled up his sleeve and showed me a tattoo on his arm. It was a woman's face, rendered so perfectly in ink that I expected her to move at any moment.

"Who's that?" I asked.

"The first person I ever killed."

I recoiled. "Really?" I looked at her again. She was young, probably only a few years older that me. Her hair was pulled back, but her face was turned slightly away, obscuring her right eye. "Was she a trader?" I asked.

He nodded. "I was seventeen. The leader of the band of rogues I was with at the time put a gun into my hand while he held her down, his boot planted firmly on her neck. She didn't cry or beg. That's what shocked me the most. She looked me straight in the eye, proud, regal. She was a queen,

Kioto, and I assassinated her."

"And why the tattoo?"

"She deserved something lasting. She deserved a lot more. I saw her face every single moment, whether my eyes were closed or not. It was more than a haunting, more than a possession. When I killed her, her soul had lifted up into me, I swear it." He tapped his temple. "She lives in here, right alongside me. Sometimes I think she's assassinating me, slowly, piece by piece. I thought this might exorcise her image from my head."

"It didn't?"

"Not at all. But you know what? I wouldn't want it to. Not now. I have to remember her. She set me on a path there was no returning from."

"And after that? Do you have them all tattooed on you?"

"In a way." He tapped the tattoo. "They all became her. Every single one of them, I saw her face. I've killed her over and over and over, and every time it feels exactly the same. So, you ask me how I can be so emotionless. I'm not. I'm just used to it, and that's the worst thing of all. So keep hold of your pain and anguish, ball it up, treasure it, if you must, but you have to make a decision and stick to it. Which consequences are worth more to you?"

59

KIOTO

When we arrived at Miyakata, we drove into the city, away from the main road to Okaporo.

"Where are they taking us?" I asked Dai.

"I do not know," he replied.

I leaned forward and tapped our driver on the shoulder. He snorted as he woke up from snoozing.

"Where are we going?" I asked.

He shrugged sleepily. "The route was pre-set, I have no idea." He lay back against the seat.

"So, what exactly is the point in having you here?" Dai asked.

The driver opened one eye and sighed deeply. "I dunno. In case there's an emergency, I guess."

"Well, thank goodness for that. You're really alert to any change in the situation, aren't you?"

The driver shrugged again and closed his eyes.

Dai turned to me and lowered his voice. "I hope he's not getting a bonus."

"Can they even call them 'drivers' anymore? They don't exactly drive an auto car."

"I suppose 'lazy bastard behind the wheel' doesn't look so good on his CV."

I suppressed a snort of laughter, turning it, not entirely successfully, into a coughing fit.

Miyakata was a city that seemed not to fully understand how cities worked. The outer ring held the suburbs; attractive streets of houses, with increasingly smaller gardens, until those houses were packed together with front doors that opened right onto the streets. Then came the tower blocks. Concrete at first, built for residency, their balconies covered in washing lines, wrapping around the buildings like bunting. Further in, the glass buildings reigned, full of enterprise and first impressions. But then, in the very centre of the city, the glass and tarmac gave way to the inner suburb of Nakoto, like a country town planted in the middle of everything else. It was green and lush, artificially so, with a rainbow mist rising from a host of sprinklers.

It was a sprawling gated community for the elite, giving them the best of both worlds. They were in the heart of the business district, but they looked out of their front windows onto expansive parkland.

The car stopped in front of an impressive building with a glass facade that rose up from the entrance, standing taller than the roof behind it. Etched into the glass were the words 'NAKOTO GUN CLUB'.

I looked at Dai.

"I guess your lesson starts here," he said.

The interior of the gun club had been air conditioned to a temperature that rose goosebumps down my arms, and sent a shiver through me. It seemed appropriate, like the inside of a tomb.

Kinawa, who had travelled in a separate car with an entourage of assistants, approached the reception desk. The woman sitting behind it slowly raised her head with a look of disdain, as if Kinawa represented a severe waste of her precious time. He said something I couldn't hear, and she nodded, buzzing the interior doors open.

"Is this necessary?" I asked, catching up with him. I placed my hand on his arm to stop him, to stall our procession towards my shooting lesson.

"Yes," he replied. "You need to look like you know what you're doing."

"Do I?"

"You're Kioto, the vessel killer, the country's hero. We can't have you looking like you've never fired a gun before."

"But I have never fired one before."

Kinawa clapped me on the shoulder. "But we don't want your fans knowing that."

"My fans?"

He gave a long, laboured sigh. "It's all about image. Let me worry about that, you just do as you're told, as per your contract." He split the last few words up, giving extraordinary weight to each of them. As if I needed reminding.

"But you said there'd be a sniper."

"That's just in case something goes horribly wrong. Kioto, this is your job, your agreement. You want to be the triumphant hero? Then shoot that vessel yourself."

60

KIOTO

The car hadn't even stopped at Okaporo before I threw the door open and tumbled out. I clambered to my feet and staggered forward, searching the blurred crowd for a familiar face. I found one, and fell into the awaiting arms.

Tian pressed his face into my hair. "I missed you so much. I've waited so long." He pushed me away, to arm's length, and looked at me. "I love you," he whispered. He held his breath, and leant forward, his eyes swimming with hope.

I pulled him back against me. "Don't ever let me go," I whimpered.

"Never. I'll never let you go again."

Another set of arms wrapped around, and the doughy body of Narata lay against me.

"Welcome home, Kioto," she said.

I threw my head back and took the deepest breath of the salty air I could. I breathed in again, I wanted to fill my lungs with it, flushing out any remnants of the prison.

"I need the sea," I said, breaking free of Tian's grip.

I half ran, half stumbled down the path to the beach, my vision obscured by tears. But my feet knew the way. They would never forget. As I stepped onto the gritty sand, I kicked off my shoes. My naked toes found their way over the coarse beach, the strip of pebbles, the stab of broken shell, until the cold water licked them. I didn't stop. I ran, fully-clothed, into the swell. And when the water reached my waist, I dropped forward and began to swim. The water embraced me. 'You're home,' it whispered with every surge. 'You're home,' screamed the gulls above me. Even the clang of the boats' bells rang out my return.

I pulled myself from the water, clothes sodden and heavy, and sat in the sand. I buried my feet in it and lay back. I closed my eyes as someone crunched across the sand towards me.

"Your sister's waiting to see you," Narata's voice said.

"Omori," I whispered, and heaved myself to my feet. "Omori."

As I ran back to the colony I could hear the tramp of the camera operators behind me, with their ragged breathing. But I ignored them, ducking out on my agreement to be aware of my angles.

They could trail around after me all they wanted, but I wasn't going to be concerned with them.

As I wrapped my arms around my sister, standing to one side of her enormous belly, I thought that I might never let her go. That we would stay like this forever, her head laid on my shoulder, my nose in her neck. I reached out and took hold of Jodo's hand. My brother-in-law. My family had expanded so much while I'd been gone, and they'd given me a home to return to, where before, I had nothing.

"Kioto," said Omori, trying to pull away from me. I held on. "Kioto," she said again.

I relented, and let her slip free of my embrace.

"Did Dai tell you that there's a vessel in Lobaya?"

"He did."

"There's something different about this one, she's not like the others."

"Different how?"

"She's less in control of her powers. Her emotions are all over the place. The others, they were always so controlled, so focussed. Single minded. But this one..." Omori paused, trying to find the right words. "It's like she's following her heart, not her head. Does that make sense?"

I nodded thoughtfully.

"I thought that maybe she was young. Untrained."

"But why would she be untrained? We know that Qathab manufacture their vessels. They're brought up as weapons. Why would she be in

Lobaya before being trained?"

"I know. It makes no sense. But I know what I felt, Kioto. She is not in control of her powers."

"Then that makes her all the more dangerous."

"What are we going to do?"

On my insistence, Kinawa shooed the cameras away, sending them off to interview Narata and the other traders. I sat on the sofa with Omori, her hands grasped in mine. Jodo's bulk filled the space by the door, arms folded, and Dai mirrored him on the other side of the room. Kinawa settled himself into the armchair, smoothing down his suit.

"Kioto is going to deal with the vessel," Kinawa said. "She'll become a national hero, and the world will be watching as she does it."

Omori looked between me and Kinawa. "How exactly is she going to 'deal with the vessel'?"

"I'm going to kill her," I said. My voice shrunk along with my shoulders.

"You are? How?"

"She's going to shoot her," Kinawa replied. "She's been trained."

Omori stared at me open-mouthed.

I shook my head at her, just a tiny movement. She closed her mouth and looked back at Kinawa. "And it's going to be broadcast?"

"Live," he said proudly.

"You're going to show an assassination on live TV? Someone actually dying?"

"The death of the enemy, the triumphant hero. It will be like nothing else."

Omori huffed. "Well, you're right there." She

looked back at me. "And you've said 'no' to this, right?"

I opened my mouth, but only managed a small groan.

"Kioto's freedom depends on it. We have a contract, and she has to follow through, or her freedom will be repealed."

Omori's mouth dropped open again.

"They own me," I said. "But it's the only reason I'm here with you now. This vessel, she's the enemy, we have to remember that."

"But she's different, Kioto. I don't think... I don't think she has the same intentions. She's innocent." Omori's hand moved to her stomach.

"And deadly," interjected Kinawa.

I shot him a warning look. "We have to remember what this vessel is capable of."

Omori struggled to her feet. "I'm capable of it too, Kioto. Are you going to kill me?" She stamped off to the bedroom, slamming the door behind her.

I dropped my head into my hands. "She's right, she's totally right."

"Either way," Kinawa said cautiously, "you need to convince her to help us. We need her to pinpoint the vessel's location."

I flung my arm towards the bedroom. "You heard her. I may as well be putting the bullet into her head." I jabbed my finger towards him. "You bloody convince her."

61

KIOTO

The bedroom was dark and stuffy. Omori lay on the bed, her feet dangling over the edge, one arm folded over her face. She groaned and rolled onto her side.

"Just leave me alone, Jodo."

I sat on the edge of the bed. "It's me."

"Go away."

"What's going on? What aren't you telling me?"

She groaned again and rolled over, slowly, turning her back to me.

"What's going on?" I asked again. "Omori."

"I'm in early labour," she muttered. "I'm in pain, so leave me be."

"Have you spoken to the midwife?"

"Yes, she came over from Iwoyo this morning."

"Where is she now?"

Omori shrugged.

"Omori, you're in labour."

"Early labour," she corrected. "It's not active labour. It could be hours and hours, days even."

"Can I do anything?"

"You can leave me alone."

I stared at the floor. "I hate it too. What they're making me do. Don't think that I actually want to do it."

"But you're going to."

"I don't have a choice."

"There's always a choice."

"Then what would you have me do, Omori? Go back to prison for something I didn't do? Never see you again, or Tian, or Okaporo? Never even get the chance to hold my nephew?"

She turned her head and stared at me. "You'll be holding him with bloodied hands."

"What is it about this vessel that makes her so precious?"

Omori turned away from me again. "She hasn't done anything wrong."

"You don't know that. And even if she hasn't yet, it doesn't mean that she won't."

"It doesn't mean I won't either."

I roared at her, exasperated. "You and her are not the same!"

Omori shrugged again. "I don't see any difference."

"Then, I don't know what to say. I don't know what to do, Omori. What would you do?"

Omori didn't answer. We sat in silence for a moment.

"Can you tell me where she is?" I asked.

"I can tell you where she's going."

"Where?"

"She's coming here. To Okaporo."

"What? Then we need to intercept her. Omori, if she gets too close to you... The baby... You need to tell us exactly where she is."

Omori nodded. "I know."

"When were you going to say something?"

"I think she started off my labour."

"What? How?"

"She didn't mean to. Something happened to make her spew out energy, emotions. They hit me and that's when the contractions started."

"Then we can't let her get any closer."

"Please don't kill her," Omori whispered.

"You need to focus on yourself. Just tell me where she is, and don't worry about it. I'll sort it."

Omori went quiet, her breathing deepening. I sat and waited.

"Omori?" I placed my hand on her shoulder and she jumped at my touch. "Don't connect for too long."

"She's almost here," Omori said.

"Where's she coming from? Which road is she on?"

Omori shook her head. "I can't see. Just wait for her."

I narrowed my eyes. I didn't believe her. In Honporo she was able to pinpoint their locations exactly, in just a few seconds. Something was wrong. I patted her arm and left her alone, closing the bedroom door behind me.

"Well?" Kinawa asked.

I ignored him and turned to Jodo. "Look after her. Don't let her leave this house. And don't let her connect to the vessel again. I'm going to find the midwife, and we're going to need a circle of traders."

"Did she tell you the vessel's location?" Kinawa asked.

"She's on her way to Okaporo. But we cannot let her get here."

I marched out of the house, Dai right behind me, and Kinawa trailing somewhere behind.

"There's something different about this vessel, and Omori's not telling me the whole truth," I said to Dai. "She wouldn't tell me where the vessel was, and she was connected for far too long. We need to stop her before she arrives."

"How can you if you don't know what direction she's coming from?"

"How many rogues are in Okaporo right now?"

"I don't know, ten, maybe twenty."

"Send them out, and make sure they're all armed. They can cover the roads."

"And what if she's coming across country? Or on a boat even?"

"Well, if she manages to slip past your rogues, then she'll be really sorry. Because that's when she'll meet us." I turned round to Kinawa. "Where's that gun of mine?"

62

OMORI

I could hear Jodo's heavy feet pacing up and down the hallway outside the door. A sentry. It didn't matter, I could go exactly where I wanted to from the confines of my bed.

I closed my eyes and reached out with my mind. Further, further, and then I grabbed hold of the vessel's jumble of thoughts, clinging tightly as they sloshed back and forth like the ocean.

"Who are you?" I asked her again.

The same flood of images spewed forth, unstructured, unintelligible.

"Slow down, I can't understand you."

The flood of thoughts quelled, but made no more sense to me. They were snippets, jumbled together with emotions.

"You need to be clearer. This is important. We're running out of time."

A single image came through then, but the emotion attached to it was nothing more than confusion. A woman's eyes, a surgical mask over the mouth, a fleck of metal on the end of a blade.

"Mother," came the vessel's own voice at last.

The next image was of a roaring bonfire on the slope of a hill, figures circling around it. Dancing. There were flags, banners, drums.

"Father."

It didn't make any sense.

"Sisters."

My breath caught as I watched image after image of Kioto, and of me. The images came faster and faster, and the emotion crashed over me, tumbling through my body, forcing the air from my lungs. Pain tore through my stomach.

"Don't come to Okaporo!" I screamed at her. "They'll kill you!" But the connection was already lost.

63

KIOTO

Despite every instruction I'd given, every insistence, even desperate pleading, Kinawa wouldn't let anyone else kill the vessel. Under his authority, the rogues that had seen her had simply stood back and watched her pass by.

"This is too good an opportunity," he had said. "The enemy coming to Okaporo, walking straight into the your home, your territory. You must do it yourself, Kioto. It will be perfect."

Unfortunately, at that point, they hadn't yet issued my gun.

They had allowed me one request, however. Dai stood by my side, his gun loaded.

If I had been simultaneously watching the live broadcast, I would have seen myself, stood in front of the colony, the Ravens Gate sign behind me. My eyes narrowed against the sun, my hair blowing back from my face, my scars displayed proudly. And next to me, the hard-set, weathered face of Dai. His eyes determined beneath greying eyebrows. Both of us stood, legs apart, guns pointed down at the floor. Kinawa had also chosen a soundtrack. Some punk song full of bass guitar and women screaming about their vaginas or something. It was the hero fantasy he'd dreamt of.

Of course, it didn't feel anything like that. Despite planting my feet heavily into the dirt, my knees shook, and it took all of my strength to stop them from collapsing under me. My hands were so slick with sweat that I could barely hold onto the gun, even against the rough grip. It felt like it might slide out from my fingers, no doubt shooting me in the leg as it hit the ground. I kept my eyes on the road ahead, but they ached to look for the sniper, search the blank windows for him, beg him to do the job for me. I didn't feel like a hero at all. I felt like a child, being asked to do something far beyond her years.

"Are you ready?" Dai whispered.

"I'll never be ready," I replied.

"Just empty your mind. Don't think, do. If you stop to think, if you hesitate at all, you won't do it."

"But that's why you're here."

"It's up to you to finish this."

I nodded. "I'm protecting Omori. That's all."

I looked up as a flash caught my attention; the sun striking the windscreen of an auto car. It pulled up and stopped. I looked at Dai.

"The rogues said she was on foot," he said.

"Maybe she got a lift."

The door opened and I moved to raise my gun,

"Wait," Dai said.

A woman uncoiled herself out of the car. Tall, elegant, controlled. Unmistakably Qathab. She looked around, her eyes finally falling on me.

"Kioto," she said.

"And you are?"

She smiled slightly. "Just here to collect my property." She turned and looked up the road. "Ah, here it comes now."

The vessel was a child, and even younger than I had expected. Barely a teenager. She was running towards us. I lifted my gun.

"Wait," Dai said again.

The vessel skidded to a halt ahead of us, loose stones flying out from under her. She looked at the Qathab woman, and then at me, and then at my gun.

"Nisa Irrin," the vessel said to the woman. "How did you find me?" She glanced down at her arm.

"Because you did the most predictable of things," Nisa Irrin replied. She looked up at me.

"You sent her to kill me," I said.

Nisa Irrin smiled her half smile again. "You think everything's so simple. Tit for tat. We all have a higher purpose, Kioto, if we care to look for it. But while we're here, perhaps we'll see." She looked back at the vessel. "Are you a defective product,

Nola?"

Nola looked at me. "No," she said. "I'm not defective."

"Then do what you were born to do," Nisa Irrin instructed.

There was shouting and screaming behind us, but I couldn't turn around. My gun was fixed on Nola. I couldn't turn around.

"Kioto!"

I couldn't turn around.

"Kioto!"

Dai's hand was on my arm. "Kioto. Omori."

I turned. My sister was scrambling towards me, one hand on the ground, the other held against her stomach. Her face was squeezed in pain, her shouts interspersed with screams and groans.

"Kioto, no!" she cried.

Jodo was there, his arms grabbed her, scooped her up, pulled her away.

"Get her out of here," I called out.

"Kioto!" Omori bellowed. "She's our sister!"

"Kill her," Nisa Irrin commanded. "Kill the murderer of our people. The murderer of your true sisters."

Nola approached, her hand reached out towards me.

"What are you going to do?" Dai asked.

"I'm not going to hesitate," I replied, and squeezed the trigger.

Nisa Irrin looked surprised as the bullet tore through one side of her face. As she dropped to her knees, her hands desperately trying to piece her head back together, she looked furious.

Pushing me aside, Dai stepped forward and put a bullet into her chest. And the silence that followed would haunt me forever. The sea held its breath in that moment, and even the gulls above us quietened.

Nola fell into my arms.

I dropped my gun and held up my hands. "She's the vessel," I cried out, pointing at Nisa Irrin's body. "She was the vessel."

I'd done my job, and they had their hero. No one cared who I'd actually killed. I looked up at Kinawa. He looked relieved. No one wanted to broadcast the death of a child, even a potentially deadly one.

"Omori," Nola said. "The baby's coming. She needs help."

64

KIOTO

I pulled back the curtains and threw the bedroom window open, sucking in a lungful of cool air.

"It's far too stuffy in here," I said.

"He'll get cold," Omori replied. She tugged at the covers, laying them over her son's tiny body.

"He needs sea air in those lungs."

"He's got a lifetime to fill his lungs with sea air."

I relented, and latched the window closed. "And is the poor little guy going to get a name any time soon?"

"Yes. I'm going to call him Saji."

"His grandfather's name. Dad would have loved that."

Omori smiled up at me. "He would. And when are you coming back? This little man needs his

Auntie Kioto cuddles."

I groaned. "Debriefings, interviews, PR, PR, PR. Can you believe I'm doing a photo shoot tomorrow? I'll get back as soon as I can." I looked down at Saji sleeping gently. "And there will be no shortage of Auntie Kioto cuddles."

"And when will you be granting him a cousin to play with?"

I laughed. "Slow down, he's only a week old, and that's the same age as my relationship with Tian. I'm not even thinking about marriage yet, and kids? I'm fine with one I can hand back for now."

"Too busy saving the world, eh?"

"Again."

She smiled. "Again." She brushed Saji's cheek, and he stirred. "One day I'll tell you 'The Legend of Kioto'. Your infamous auntie."

"And what about his other auntie?"

Omori tapped her forehead. "We can never get close. Having her walk into Okaporo almost killed me. But when he's older, I'm sure he'll love having holidays in Iwoyo with her."

"At least you can talk with her whenever you need to."

Omori nodded. "She's really learning to control her abilities. Narata's doing really good work with her."

I clapped my hands together. "I'd better get going."

"You look tired, Kioto. Are you still having nightmares?"

"Don't worry about it." I bent and kissed Saji's

head. "Look after your mummy for me, I'll be back soon."

Dai was already waiting in the car outside. "Ready?" he asked, leaning out of the open door.

"Just give me a minute," I said.

I followed the path down the side of Omori's house and stepped out onto the open grass beyond. Tian was sitting on his bench, watching the sea. I sat next to him.

"I'm off now," I said.

"I'll miss you," he replied.

I kissed him. "I'll miss you too." I looked out over the water. "Look after Okaporo for me."

"Marry me," he said.

"Maybe one day." I stood up. "Once I'm finally free to be myself again."

"They'll find a new hero soon enough."

I shrugged. "Probably."

"In the meantime, all of this will be waiting for you."

I smiled. "The world doesn't wait for anyone."

THE SISTER

ACKNOWLEDGEMENTS

Once again, I find myself struggling in the reality of how restrictive our language is in comparison to the gratitude I need to express.

As ever, the top of my list is my husband, Paul, my sounding board, my anchor, my lighthouse when I get lost in the sea of my creative temperament. You're always there to lead me back to shore, to set me back on solid land (which you know is exactly where I feel the safest).

Our beautiful boys who are everything, and the very soul of our family. They may not be overly helpful with the actual writing (peace and quiet is in very short supply round here), but when my five year old begins to really understand what I do for a living, and says "Oh my God, Mummy, I'm so proud of you," it reminds me of why I do this. He did, however, continue with "because you write books and because you smell," but, hey, he's five. I can't expect poetry from him yet.

My wonderful parents who have always encouraged my love of words and my belief in magic. My extraordinarily busy sister who, I know, will get around to reading this one day. She's been a huge champion of my writing from the start, and has lost a few copies of my books to friends and colleagues who begged her copy from her.

The all-important eyes of Kay Smillie, Pat Salvant, Riddhi Padwal, and Alina Hart. You're worth your weight in gold, and you probably don't even realise how much I value your input.

My cover designer, Olivia, who didn't even need a second pass at this cover.

My peers and fellow writers who have helped in ways they won't even realise. It's amazing how much difference one encouraging comment can make, or the response of someone who truly understands the problems writers have. I can be myself with them, and nerd out with them, and they'll never laugh at my addiction to pretty notebooks, and they understand the importance of a great-smelling book.

And you, my readers, the people who allow my characters to live on after I've finished writing about them.

ABOUT ANGELINE TREVENA

Angeline Trevena was born and bred in a rural corner of Devon, but now lives among the breweries and canals of central England with her husband, their two sons, and a rather neurotic cat. She is a horror and fantasy author, poet, and journalist.

In 2003 she graduated from Edge Hill University, Lancashire, with a BA Hons Degree in Drama and Writing. During this time she decided that her future lay in writing words rather than performing them.

Some years ago she worked at an antique auction house and religiously checked every wardrobe that came in to see if Narnia was in the back of it. She's still not given up looking for it.

Find out more at www.angelinetrevena.co.uk